Sanctuary

Chelsea's Story

The Carpenter Chronicles: Book Two
A Christian Romance

Janice Limb Myers

©2014 LJM Publishing and Janice Limb Myers

All International Rights Reserved

ISBN 978-0-9861946-0-3 ebook
ISBN 978-0-9861946-1-0 paperback

Cover Photo Credits

Shutterstock #9283960
Shutterstock #98613266

Dear Reader,

Thank you for purchasing this, the second book in *The Carpenter Chronicles*. The Carpenters are a family whose faith in God and Jesus Christ sees them through life's trials and tribulations. This series contains six books, one for each of the living family members. Just a few snippets about the family:

• John Carpenter died four years ago in a skiing accident in Deer Valley, Utah. He was an accomplished skier.

• Grace Carpenter took over running the family publishing business after John's death and has gallantly fulfilled her role as the matriarch of the family.

• Carrie, Chelsea, Carter and Cassie are John and Grace's natural children. Courtney was adopted into the family at age 7. Chelsea and Carter are twins. Chelsea and Courtney work in the family publishing business. Carrie is a journalist in New York and Carter is an architect in San Francisco. Cassie is a novelist.

As each book progresses and others are added to the family, you will see the family tree change. I hope you enjoy the Carpenters as much as I'm enjoying writing about them. M promise to you are good, clean stories devoid of bad language or sex scenes, with characters who acknowledge their faith in God and demonstrate good Christian values in spite of challenges they face.

Again my thanks, and happy reading!

Janice Limb Myers

DEDICATION

To all who have loved and lost.

"The price of great love is great misery when one of you dies."
Lord Grantham, *Downton Abbey*

THE CARPENTER

JOHN GRACE CARRIE COURTENAY CASSIE CHELSEA CARTER

FAMILY TREE

BOOK TWO

CHAPTER ONE

Chelsea's mind was already on Clark as she stepped out onto the deck dressed in her bathrobe, carrying a cup of hot chocolate. This was a ritual begun the first morning she had awakened in her new condo high in the mountains above Sundance.

Raising her cup toward the sky, she smiled as she announced, "Good morning, Clark," as though he was there to hear her. In quiet times such as this her mind filled with precious memories of their time together and thoughts of what might have been.

Her reverie was too soon interrupted with the thought that she still needed to hit the shower and get ready for work. The CEO had scheduled a meeting for 9 a.m. and there was plenty of work sitting on Chelsea's desk that required her attention before that meeting.

"So I propose we consolidate the marketing division under one department head in order to maximize efficiency and allow for the more effective and efficient use of shared resources."

Chelsea Carpenter tapped her pen on the legal pad that sat on the boardroom table in front of her as she listened to her mother's closing statement. Grace had made a sound argument, but Chelsea still had a few questions.

"So what happens to the current heads of the individual departments? Does that mean they are demoted or reassigned elsewhere?"

"Of course not, Chelsea. Each department will run as usual, and the people will retain their positions. My vision is for all the departments as a whole to be coordinated by one person, rather than coming to the board for everything.

"So you're proposing handing over a lot of power with this position?" Charles asked.

Charles had served on the board of directors for as long as Chelsea could remember, working side-by-side with her father up until that fateful day five years ago. They were all grateful he had continued to be the loyal right-hand man for her mother, just as he had always been for her father.

"Yes, I am proposing handing over a great deal of authority," Grace answered Charles. "I think it's about time the board didn't have to vote on quite so many decisions involved in the day-to-day management of the firm.

"I know John wanted to be involved in everything in a major way, but that can still be achieved without hampering timelines and creativity. I have kept his procedures in place for five years; now I think it's time for change."

"What about the additional cost of external hiring? Wouldn't it be more cost effective to promote from within?"

"Short-term perhaps it would be, Chelsea, but I feel that the internal upheaval would slow down current projects and interfere with deadlines. The teams that are in place in each department work very well at the moment, and I don't think it's sensible to upset that balance.

"The new member of the staff should be an asset to them all, an extra benefit to relieve some of their workload, and I think everyone would be happier with that arrangement if the person chosen came from outside and had no particular loyalties to any one department. Long-term I think it's the most viable financial as well as operational option," Grace replied.

Chelsea watched several members of the board nod in agreement. It was a bold move by her mother, changing the way her father had run things, but she agreed—it was time.

No one had any further questions, so her mother wrapped up the meeting and the board agreed to meet at the same time the following day to cast their votes. Chelsea made her way back to her office to consider her position on the matter.

"Good meeting?" her personal assistant, Beth, asked as she stepped into the outer office.

"Interesting," Chelsea said. "Looks like we're injecting new blood into Marketing. Do I have any appointments for the rest of the day?"

"No appointments, but three deadlines to meet, and the slush pile of manuscripts has grown ten-fold."

"Doesn't it always?" Chelsea laughed. "Okay, I'm going to go and hunker down in there and get those deadlines met, then spend a bit of time thinking over what Mom proposed today before we vote tomorrow. Can you hold all calls unless something's really urgent?"

"Sure thing, I'll handle everything. Just buzz me if you need anything."

The women smiled at each other. After working together for a year, they had become a tight-knit unit; and Chelsea knew she could trust and rely on Beth, and Beth knew she had a great boss and a great position.

The mutual respect kept the relationship working perfectly in the office environment, allowing their friendship to blossom without it altering their working dynamic. Chelsea walked past Beth and stepped into her inner sanctum, closing the door behind her.

She instantly felt comforted by her surroundings. Two of the pale blue walls were covered in floor to ceiling shelving which contained piles of manuscripts, neatly typed (for the most part). Some were even hand-scrawled, more like random thoughts than a well-constructed piece of fiction, all held together by giant bulldog clips and stacked in various sections according to their current place in the process.

She walked over to her French antique writing desk she had purchased in memory of her father who had used a similar desk for many years. Thoughts of her dad filled her mind as she ran her fingers along the pale green leather top embossed with gold. She had been just 21 years old when her father died.

Sitting down in her battered but comfortable chair, she picked up the first of the sci-fi novels already laid on her desk by the ever-efficient Beth. Sci-fi wasn't really her thing; as chief editor of the romance section she requested the transfer to sci-fi just over two years ago.

After what happened, she just couldn't handle spending each day working on romance novels.

Over time, she worked to develop a deep understanding of the genre and its oft-hidden comparisons and parables. She had always been able to do her job, recognizing good writing and clever plots when she came across them. Now that she'd acquired a genuine love for the material she was working with, she could really enjoy her work again.

As chief editor, the material had already been copy-edited by a member of her team and sent back to the author for revision—perhaps several times—but it was her job to check over and approve the final draft before it went for proofreading and typesetting for publication.

Undoing the massive clip, she turned over the first page of the manuscript and settled down to read.

Two hours later, she turned the final page and sat back, rubbing her hazel eyes. She had only found two small sections she wanted to change, so she'd made the notes in the wide margins as she went.

She decided she would check with the author and made the call. After the changes had been agreed upon, she pulled up the document onscreen and applied the tiny touches of magic she felt it needed.

Satisfied, she sent the final draft to proofing; they would print it again there, adding the coded instructions for the typesetters. Stamping the manuscript with her large black stamp was immensely satisfying, and she stared at the bold capital letters on the cover page stating "COMPLETED" for a moment before placing it in the filing tray and moving on to the next.

Grace and Charles were still in the boardroom going over the finer points of the contract and the recruitment advertisement they would run for the new position.

"Charles, we have no guarantees that the board will vote in favor of my proposal, considering the significant additional cost of the position when salary, bonuses, benefits, possible moving allowances, and all the rest were added in, they felt it best to be prepared. I'd like to be ready to move quickly if the board agrees."

"It's already Thursday, Grace, and I don't have to remind you that you'll be out of the office next week for your gathering of the Carpenter clan."

"Yes, it's been a bear to pull together with the various jobs and locations of all the family members spanning from New York City to San Francisco and points in between," she laughed.

Grace had managed to pull it off, getting everyone's agreement for the upcoming weekend plus the following three working days to make it a five-day vacation for them all. They would begin traveling as early as they could on Friday night, arriving any time from within the hour to sometime on Saturday.

"I need to ensure everything is wrapped up here at the office before the weekend so the recruitment drive can begin immediately upon my return."

She smiled at the thought of having all her children home for the first time in what felt like ages. They were all so busy now with their separate lives that get-togethers were almost impossible.

She was anxious to be finished with work so she could concentrate on the arrangements for the celebration on Saturday night. She had a million and one things to do. Her smile faded a little as she considered the nature of the party.

"What's wrong, Grace?" Charles had been quick to note the change in mood of his dear friend and co-worker.

Charles had temporarily taken the helm of the business while Grace had struggled to come to terms with her husband's death, stepping aside easily when she found the strength to take her place at the head of the board. He was without a doubt a man who held the trust and admiration of the Carpenter Family, his personal concern for Grace very evident.

"Oh nothing really, I'm just a bit worried about Chelsea and how she's going to handle the weekend."

"Of course," Charles said, "the official engagement party for Carrie and Antonio. Don't you think she'll be happy for them?"

The engagement hadn't really been a low-profile event—it was broadcast on live TV in many countries across the world. So Chelsea already knew her sister's thrilling news, but none of them had met her fiancé yet.

In fact, all of them had only seen them together as a couple for more than a few enchanting minutes on the small screen. Their fairytale engagement seemed to be big news across the country, but not bigger than in Carrie's home state of Utah where replays of the live event in Madrid had aired on new broadcasts for days.

"Yes, of course, Chelsea's absolutely delighted for Carrie, and she keeps telling me she's looking forward to it, but I'm worried that actually seeing her sister in love with her new man by her side and holding the party at the house might just be too much."

"It's been two years," Charles said softly, patting Grace's hand. "I'm sure she's on the road to recovery and will handle it just fine."

Grace shook her head. "I'm not so sure, Charles. Think about it. Only three years ago, she was in exactly the same position as Carrie is now, newly engaged to her handsome soldier, celebrating that union with her friends and family at the house, their whole young lives ahead of them, plans and dreams to fulfil.

"They'd been together less than eight months when Clark was killed in Iraq, and I don't know if she'll ever get over it. Between her aunt, her father, and Clark, she's seen too many relationships end in tragedy. She might seem fine on the outside, but think about it—what has she done since then?"

Charles' face filled with pain as he realized the truth of Grace's words. "Work," he replied.

"Exactly," Grace agreed. "She moved away from her beloved romance department despite loving the genre all her life and she threw herself into work in a department she hadn't previously shown any interest in.

"When she's not here, she's holed up in her condominium at Sundance working even more. She might seem fine, but really, she's shut us all out. You know she insists on going through all the unsolicited manuscripts herself?

"Beth told me she takes a pile home with her every night. Is that any kind of life for a young woman?"

"No, it's not," Charles said. "You're absolutely right, of course—and I should have seen it for myself—but she has thrown herself into this business since she was about twelve years old, when she used to come on weekends and help out as a runner or anything else she could do.

She was always asking questions, watching how each department worked. I guess I didn't notice that her natural dedication to the business was being pushed a step too far."

"Charles, don't blame yourself. You've been an amazing mentor to Chelsea all her life, and to be honest, a father figure since John died. You're right in that she has always shown her love for the business, and the changes in her are probably something only a mother would notice.

"I'm sure it will work out; I'll have time to talk with her on Friday before the others arrive. Well, let's get back to work; I want someone amazing for this new position!"

Charles patted Grace on the shoulder and they resumed their discussion on how to word the instructions to the headhunter to attract exactly the right candidates.

CHAPTER TWO

Chelsea stood staring out the window, listening to the majestic Stewart Falls as the water powered its way down the beautifully imposing Mt. Timpanogos. Her condo high in the mountains was perfectly placed to give her the constant sounds of the waterfall rushing all the way down to the famous Sundance Theatre and beyond.

It was the ultimate back yard—an impressive display of the beauty of nature and a perfect example of how it could be enjoyed fully without being spoiled. The view was a constant reminder that directly on the other side of this mountain was the Mt. Timpanogos Temple, the planned site of her marriage to Clark.

Her condo had been built using natural materials, designed to blend into and enhance the mountainside rather than marring the landscape. The clever use of glass brought the outdoors inside every room, each one a perfect mix of modern living laid out among rough, natural wood, slate, and stone.

Chelsea had loved the place when she first viewed it, and in her weaker moments, she allowed herself to admit how romantic a setting it actually was. She had even once heard an old legend that if two people managed to cross the run-off from the falls without touching the water or getting wet, they would be in love forever.

I don't need any myths to help me fall in love forever, she thought. *I've already done that. And just because Clark is no longer around doesn't mean I don't still love him with all my heart.*

She walked to the recliner and sat to enjoy a few minutes of relaxation before packing for the family staycation.

If I'm being honest with myself, she thought, *I told people I chose this home for its rustic charm and the beautiful surroundings, but in reality it was the isolation that drew me to it.*

After losing Clark, she wanted to lose herself too. Whether in books or up in her nest in the mountains where no one would ever seek her out, her plan worked.

Located high in the mountains between Heber City and Provo, nobody bothered her here. In two years she had never invited a family member or a friend to her hideout.

There were never any sales people knocking on doors, nobody visited because they were just passing by, and it was the perfect retreat for someone who wanted to cut herself off from the world by creating a sanctuary no one else would enter. After all, grief far outlasts sympathy.

She'd known there was no quick way to get over the pain; she wanted to be alone with it, wanted to cry and scream and yell in private, wanted to walk around, talking to Clark whenever she felt like it.

She didn't need people telling her to snap out of it or get over it, or offer constant platitudes and tell her what a great guy he had been.

She just needed to get it all out and then close off her emotional side. Between the isolated apartment and the move to the sci-fi, she felt she had done it quite successfully. And both Grace and Charles understood why she had to move from the romance department.

She had to admit that it hadn't been an easy task. All of the Carpenter girls were raised on romance and tales of happily-ever-afters. They had been girly girls, loving anything in pink or purple, frills and sparkles, and fairytales, hoping for their handsome prince or brave knight to come along and whisk them off on a faithful stallion.

Well, Chelsea had found her brave knight, or rather her soldier. He was everything she had ever wanted, and then he was taken away from her before they got their chance of a life together. There was no one to blame for it; it was what it was. True love had been found and it had been lost, end of story.

Chelsea sighed and walked back to her bed, where she had laid out her items to pack. That was as far as she'd gotten with her preparations for the short vacation.

She was excited about it, though; she loved going home and couldn't wait to see her family, especially her twin brother Carter. Not to mention she was overjoyed for Carrie and couldn't wait to meet Antonio. *Trust Carrie to end up with her love life not only plastered all over the newspapers, but broadcast on live television!*

Her eldest sister was what Chelsea thought of as accident-prone in terms of her love life, always picking the wrong guys or getting herself into crazy situations on dates. She had been a source of amusement to them all throughout their late teens and college years.

Chelsea wondered if living in New York and working for a true-blue New York editor had changed Carrie. Would she be tougher, more hard-nosed and worldly-wise, or would she still be the sweet and slightly naïve sister she remembered?

Journalism had been a strange choice of career for Carrie, but her path was now clear to her family, as it led her to Antonio, her very own prince. It was so true that God worked in mysterious ways, and it was not for the likes of us to question, she reaffirmed to herself.

She still thanked Him every day for the time she and Clark had together—every second a blessing, every fleeting moment a life-enhancing experience that she would never forget. Her broken heart would see to that.

She was grateful each day, however, for her faith that kept her going, knowing families are forever;

even though she and Clark did not have the opportunity to be a family, she believed they would see each other again in the eternities.

Until then, she had her family, her work, her faith, and her lovely shelter from the world in which to live.

Her thoughts brought her back to her unfinished packing. She had to admit she felt a slight sense of trepidation about the engagement party. She remembered her own so well, the huge marquees outside in the impressive grounds of her home, archways of flowers and every tree decorated with twinkle lights, the décor silver and blue to match her outfit.

Oh, how she and Clark had danced that night! She remembered how her feet ached so she took off her slippers and danced barefoot across the lush green grass, savoring its cool softness.

Clark's strong arms swung her round in graceful sweeps as they abandoned the dance floor that had been laid out across the grass for the night. She also remembered sitting with him, dangling her feet in the pool after the party, gently sweeping them through the soothing water. She was wrapped in his embrace, talking of their plans for their next milestone, their wedding day.

"Enough!" she told herself firmly. "Get a move on and get packing."

She walked to her closet and picked out suitable outfits for a variety of activities the siblings might want to do together during their stay. After carefully folding and packing the clothes, she looked at the pile of manuscripts that sat on her nightstand beckoning to her.

She hesitated, then picked them up and added them to the large backpack. *Just in case I can't handle celebrating with the happy couple. Get a grip!* Organized but perhaps not fully mentally prepared, she grabbed her keys and headed for her car.

The drive into Midway was a fairly short one once she got down the steep mountain road to the highway. She especially loved the sounds of the water flowing down from the falls that cascaded along the side of the pavement as she drove.

The surrounding scenery provided a pleasant backdrop as she traveled. The trees and flowers were beginning to blossom, creating a riot of beauty, and the highway ran through the canyon following the furiously surging Provo River, infused by whitecaps from the overflow of spring runoff coming through Deer Creek Reservoir.

She let the stunning natural magnificence of the views soothe her and allowed her excitement at seeing all her family together take over her thoughts.

It wasn't long before she was traveling up the driveway of the thirty-acre homestead toward the house. The French country buildings came into view as the driveway split into a fork, one direction leading to a large circular drive at the front of the house, the other leading to the garages and horse barn at the rear.

She made her way slowly past the house, heading for the garages. Being home again always brought a measure of peace to her heart.

After parking her car, she walked down to the stables and greeted the horses. They whickered gently and pressed their velvety muzzles against her hands and chest, welcoming her back and nuzzling for treats.

She felt a crack in her heart armor as she stroked the gentle but majestic beasts. She loved to ride, and it had been too long. Promising herself she would find time over the next five days, she said goodbye to her old friends and walked around to the back of the house.

As she entered the door from the patio into the massive family room, she was immediately overwhelmed by three female figures rushing up to hug her. Laughing, she tried to stretch her arms around all of them at once. *I've missed these group hugs!*

"We heard the car! It's great to see you. We may work in the same place, but we hardly ever get to spend time together!" Courtney said.

"Oh, it's wonderful to have you home for a while, I've missed you," cried Maggie, a family member if ever there was one. Others may have thought of Maggie as just the housekeeper, but the Carpenters all knew otherwise.

"I missed you all, too! It's wonderful to see you," Chelsea replied, stepping back to take a good look at them.

Her mother just smiled at her, her blonde hair streaked with the odd strand of silver grey piled high in an up-do, her blue eyes shining with excitement.

Slender and always elegant, Grace was the picture of the perfect hostess, composed and demure.

Beside her stood Maggie, the housekeeper who had been hired just over thirty years ago to help the newly-married Grace learn how to run such a large household and to show her how to plan and execute the perfect business dinner party. The older woman and her husband Nigel had been invaluable to the young couple just starting out in life and in business, and they'd been with them ever since. They were considered family now, living in a house on the grounds and always being on hand for them.

Maggie was a small, round woman with grey hair and rosy cheeks, infinitely cuddly and huggable. Chelsea couldn't remember a day when Maggie hadn't been around for them during their upbringing.

Then there was Courtney, the baby of the bunch at 22. She still lived at home but worked within the firm as a junior copy editor, hoping someday to head up a branch far away from Utah.

Courtney was their little rebel, their cousin whom her parents had been adopted after the death of her mother, Chelsea's Aunt Lucy, at the age of seven.

Courtney's blonde hair was cut into a wild, spiky pixie cut. Huge, chocolate brown eyes that stared out from her small features set her apart from the rest of the family. They all thought the biggest difference was her adventurous, devil-may-care spirit. Chelsea couldn't wait to hear the stories of what Courtney had been up to lately.

As they were about to settle down to talk, the front door opened and Cassie and Nigel strolled in together. "Anybody home?" Cassie yelled. "Let the party begin, 'cause Cassie's here!"

As always, Cassie was casual in jeans, sneakers, and a sweater, her dirty blonde hair a wild and messy cascade around her. Chelsea grinned at her as Cassie walked up and nudged her. It was Cassie's way of saying hello.

"Thought I heard someone upsetting my horses," Cassie joked.

"At least they were pleased to see me," Chelsea joked back, teasing her sister.

Cassie was far from bohemian, but as an aspiring author, she loved to play the role. She dressed down, lived in the guesthouse across the pool area from the main house, holed up in an upstairs room she had turned into her office.

Chelsea had no doubt that if coffee, cigarettes, and whisky were permitted in their religion, Cassie would try them all just to see how they fit into her romanticized image of the proverbial lonely, starving artist living in a garret! She snorted at the image in her head.

Her sister was actually quite staid and solid with a strong work ethic. She was in love with the images portrayed by old black-and-white movies—writers hammering away on old style, round-keyed manual typewriters, their first lines full of dark and stormy nights or private eyes watching from high windows as dames crossed the street, barely visible through thick fog.

"What's so funny?" Cassie demanded.

"You, you great pretender. Written anything decent yet?" Chelsea asked over her shoulder as she went to greet Nigel who had been hanging around the door, unwilling to interrupt the reunion.

As always, the tall, reserved, grey-haired man had stayed dressed in his smart suit, unwilling to end his working day while there was a chance he could offer his services as a chauffeur. He had been so happy back in the days when John had allowed him to be his driver, taking his pick from the small, modest collection of classic cars that John started before his untimely demise.

Nigel obviously hoped someone would need to be picked up, or at least need him to park the cars. Chelsea gave him a warm hug, leading him into the bosom of the family group where he belonged.

"Come on, let's all go and sit down. I want to hear how everyone is doing and what you've been up to," she declared, making her way back into the large family room.

After the group had settled, Chelsea looked around them expectantly. "Come on, who's going first?"

"I've almost finished my third novel in the series," Cassie said hesitantly. "I think it's going pretty well."

"Pretty well?" Courtney interjected. "Now that's an understatement. The first was awesome. It's already on sale and getting great reviews for a first-time author.

"A little bit of marketing magic and I'm sure we can hit a list or two with it. The second is currently in production, but I've read it of course, and I loved it too. I have very high hopes for the third."

"No pressure then," Cassie said, feigning worry.

"Don't worry, with your writing talent and my editing skills, we're a force to be reckoned with," Courtney grinned at Cassie.

"You really should read them, Chels," she said, using the nickname Courtney had given her cousin-turned-sister when she was little.

Chelsea dropped her head, instantly ashamed that she hadn't supported her sister as fully as she would've liked.

Cassie's writing was firmly embedded within the romance genre, and since losing Clark, Chelsea just hadn't been able to face up to the happiness of others, especially not in the perfect world of fiction.

The room had gone quiet as each of them waited for Chelsea's response. Chelsea felt the wave of love and understanding surrounding her as she said to Cassie, "I'm so sorry, Sis."

Cassie instantly rushed to her side, putting an arm around her shoulders. "Don't be, I understand. You'll read them one day. With every one, I'm putting aside a hardback copy, signing it just for you."

Tears pricked Chelsea's eyes at the depth of love she felt emanating from her family, but she couldn't help but laugh through the tears when her sister removed her arm and gave her a firm poke in the side.

"Consider yourself lucky—those signed first-run copies will definitely be worth a fortune one day when I'm super famous!"

The comment had the desired effect, lightening the mood and moving the conversation away from the painful subject. The next few hours passed happily in a whirlwind of excited chatter before they all decided they should go to bed and try to get some sleep; they had an early start in the morning, and everyone would be pitching in with the preparations for the party that night.

As Chelsea stepped into her childhood bedroom, she silently thanked her mom for not changing a thing; it was exactly as she'd left it. The walls were a sky blue, her favorite color, accented with cream and a hint of gold in the heavy brocade drapes and pelmets that encased the dual aspect windows.

The furniture was typical French country, solid construction of heavy wood but painted in creams and off-whites, softening the look. She smiled as she recalled the times she'd sat on her bed and dreamed she was high in the sky, flying through the white fluffy clouds that puffed across the expanse of blue on a magic carpet.

What a silly, fanciful child you were, she scolded herself as she laid her backpack down on the bed and began to unpack.

A light knock on her door interrupted her.

"Come in."

She turned to see her mother slip gracefully into her room. "Can we have a chat?"

"Sure, come and sit here," Chelsea replied, moving her backpack off the bed. She sat down, patting the area beside her. Her mom obliged, edging in close so their shoulders touched.

"I wanted to make sure you were alright after that comment of Courtney's."

"Thanks, Mom, I appreciate how you all tiptoe around me, but I'm fine, honestly. And before you ask," she raised her brows, "yes, I'll be fine tomorrow."

"I see you anticipated my next question," Grace laughed softly.

"Yeah, you're totally busted," Chelsea said with a rueful smile. "I knew you'd worry about whether I could handle tomorrow, so it just followed that we'd have this conversation.

"I've wondered myself, but I'm so pleased for Carrie that I'm sure I'll be fine. I can't be jealous of my own sister, can I?"

"It wouldn't be jealousy and well you know it!" Grace exclaimed. "It would be grief over what you lost, not resenting your sister for her happiness.

"Everyone would understand if you don't attend the actual party; same place, same faces, same words being said. It's completely acceptable for you to bow out of the big celebration and just spend time with Carrie and Antonio in quieter moments."

"Thanks, Mom, but I want to be there for the sake of the family and the happy couple. I already let the business down by having to shift departments, and I'm letting Cassie down by not being able to read her books. I just can't let Carrie down, too."

"You're not letting anyone down, darling. You're doing a great job in your new department and have been responsible for signing some great, diverse new authors.

As for Carrie, you know how much she hurt for you when it all happened. She loves you very much. You two wouldn't be able to tease and poke fun at each other the way you do if you didn't love each other."

Chelsea laughed at the thought of her little sister. "Yeah, what's up with her living in that guesthouse when there are plenty of empty bedrooms here in the house?"

"She's just finding herself, that's all. She hasn't quite decided who it is she wants to be yet, and she's exploring her options." They both laughed.

"Still, her writing is showing a progressing maturity. I wouldn't be surprised if she flies the nest soon, like most of my other little chicks. So for the moment, I'm delighted that she's taken up residence out there. At least she's nearby."

The two women chuckled, and Chelsea gave her mom a spontaneous hug. Working together and both being on the board of directors, Chelsea often felt the dynamics between them had changed to a boss and employee relationship. But here, back in her beloved home, she could become the daughter again.

"Thanks for the chat, Mom, and for thinking about me. But I'm okay. It's a comfort to know I can disappear if I absolutely have to, rather than ruining the party for everyone."

"It's good to have you home. Night night, dear. Sweet dreams."

"You too, Mom. See you in the morning," Chelsea called as her mom left the room. Once again alone with her thoughts, she finished her unpacking, said her prayers, and then snuggled into bed with one of the manuscripts, hoping to find the hidden gem among the rough.

CHAPTER THREE

Chelsea was already in the kitchen with Grace and Maggie at 7 a.m. making preparations for the celebrations that would begin late afternoon. Despite the early hour, the house and grounds were already teeming with people.

Large trucks were busy delivering flowers by the armful, people were climbing up ladders to decorate even the highest trees, and caterers were already rushing around commandeering the refrigerators and freezers.

Although they would mostly cater the party, Grace still wanted to add her personal touch, including family favorites and traditions from when the kids were young.

"What time is Carter getting here?" Chelsea asked.

"He said if there were no delays he would be arriving around eight, so within the next couple of hours," Grace replied.

The grin on Chelsea's face said it all; she absolutely couldn't wait to see her twin brother. He had been both the bane of her life and her hero throughout her childhood. She sometimes felt sorry for him being surrounded by so many girls, but her dad made sure they always had at least some 'man time' together every weekend—ball games, fishing trips, skiing trips.

Her smile faded as she thought of the last skiing trip her father had ever taken. Thankfully Carter hadn't been with their dad that day. Her dad had taken a group of business associates he had been courting to an exclusive cabin at the Stein Erikson Ski Resort in Deer Valley.

He hadn't been far from home, only up above Park City, but it may as well have been a million miles away. The coroner couldn't say if the heart attack caused the fall, or if the fall brought on the heart attack, but either way, the head trauma he suffered when he hit the tree at high speed would have killed him instantly.

Nobody had been worried about him when he left that day for the short trip; he was an accomplished skier who had been brought up on those slopes. Then he was just…gone.

Chelsea felt eyes on her and she glanced up to see her mom and Maggie looking at her with pained expressions on their faces. She shook her head, clearing it of her depressing thoughts, and focused on the canapés she was making that were a favorite of Carter's.

The two women probably thought she had been thinking of Clark, and it was best if they continued to believe that. Today was not a day to tell her mother she had been thinking of Dad.

"What about the guests of honor?" she asked instead.

"Carrie thought their flight would land around eleven, and of course Nigel said he wanted to be the one to pick them up at the airport. In fact, he can't wait," Grace laughed.

"If the flight's on time and they don't take too long to collect their luggage, they should be here by noon."

"I wonder which car he'll choose. What do you think, Maggie?"

"Probably the fastest one; he's so eager to see Carrie!"

"What about Simone? Is she coming tonight?"

"Yes," Grace said firmly. "And all three of them are attending strictly as guests. Do you hear me, Maggie? No working! There are enough people here to handle everything without you, Nigel, and your lovely daughter working.

I want the three of you to sit back and enjoy the party." With hands on her hips, she put on that tough corporate look of hers, trying to appear intimidating, but Maggie and Chelsea could see beyond it and shared a knowing look with each other, then burst out laughing.

With the conversation firmly on more pleasant ground, the women continued to work in good spirits until a handsome face atop a tall, muscular body burst into the kitchen and made a grab for Chelsea, picking her up and spinning her around.

She squealed like an alarm ringing through the entire house. As she was planted firmly back on the floor, she looked up at the deep brown hair and hazel eyes that were practically a mirror image of her own. *My eyes used to shine with laughter that same way….*

"Hey Bro, it's good to see you," she said, hugging Carter quickly before releasing him to go terrorize the other two women in the same way.

"Oh, it's so good to be home! This kitchen smells fantastic already," Carter exclaimed, grabbing a handful of delicacies from the counter and stuffing them into his mouth.

"Hey, those are for later!" Chelsea complained.

"Too bad, I'm starving; the food they served on the plane wouldn't feed a sparrow. Besides, you can't deny that you're making them just for me, right?"

"Well, I guess I was making them for you, yes."

"There you go then, I'm eating them. What more do you want?"

"How about waiting until the ingredients are actually put together and baked in the oven?"

"Why wait when you can have what you want right now?"

"You're impossible," Chelsea grumbled, tempted to grab a handful of flour and throw it at her brother. She resisted, knowing a massive food fight would ensue, causing her mother to fly into a panic and probably prompting the caterers to quit on the spot!

She remembered a time when their mom came home as she and her friends were making cookies to take to the younger girls in their youth group at church. They called themselves the Young Women's Visiting Teachers, and every month they visited each of the younger girls and took them a treat.

Her mom's attention immediately went to the commotion in the kitchen as she walked in the back door. She took one look at the flour fight going on and ran straight to her bedroom to grab the camera.

The girls were all afraid they were in big trouble and couldn't believe they didn't get yelled at. What a cool mom to just take pictures. Of course, she made them clean it all up so Maggie wouldn't have to.

"Chelsea, why don't you and Carter go out into the gardens and check on what's happening? I'm still unsure if it will be warm enough to hold the whole event outside; April can be quite changeable. See if the party planner has an accurate forecast and make sure the dining room is decorated too, just in case. Maggie and I will finish up in here."

"Sure, Mom, no problem," Chelsea said, quickly washing and drying her hands before wrapping the crook of her arm inside Carter's and giving him another quick snuggle.

"So, how's San Francisco?" Chelsea asked as they made their way to the yard.

"It's okay, I guess. The city is awesome, such an amazing vibe, and I love my job, but there's nowhere quite like home, is there?"

"No, there isn't," Chelsea agreed as they both stared at the stunning mountain scenery surrounding their house. She turned her attention to the initial preparations. Large tables were being placed under the exacting instruction of a fussy man dressed in a red jumpsuit with flared bottoms, accompanied by a canary yellow cravat—obviously the flamboyant party planner.

He seemed to be continually waving his hands around and placing one, palm out, on his forehead in a dramatic gesture of horror.

"I didn't know Mom hired entertainment. What do you think, a tribute act to a headliner at Woodstock maybe?" Carter muttered, with a teasing grin.

Chelsea giggled. "Carter, don't! He's probably just…creative and artistic," she finished helplessly. "It makes no difference anyway; he's the party planner and as long as he makes the place look fabulous and is pleasant to work with, that's all that matters."

"Not looking too pleasant to work with at the moment, I'm afraid," Carter replied, as the man practically stamped his foot as he delivered a barrage of insults to the men delivering and setting up the tables, obviously not to his satisfaction. "I wonder where Mom found this one."

"Probably on someone's recommendation, so he must be good, but it's too early to tell. Come on, Handsome, let's ask about the weather and the dining room."

"Do we have to?" Carter pretended to complain, mocking his former 6-year-old style.

"I'm afraid so. Look, I'll make a deal with you. We handle this quickly and make sure everything's in order, then we'll fit in a quick ride together. What do you say?"

"Oh, now you're talking. Deal!" Carter exclaimed as he stepped up toward the small man, interrupting his tantrum with aplomb.

The entire family had changed clothes and gathered together in the family room, anxiously awaiting Nigel's arrival with the honored guests.

Despite the seemingly unprofessional manner of the party planner, the house and gardens looked absolutely resplendent in their finery.

"It looks terrific, Mom. I can't believe it all came together so quickly. What made you choose red and gold?"

"I took my inspiration from the coat of arms for the Spanish royal family." Grace left unspoken the fact that she had also wanted to choose something as far away from the glittering blues and silvers of Chelsea's own engagement party as she could find.

"Oh, isn't that a bit of a risk since he isn't really considered royalty anymore? He might be offended."

"It's a risk, I have to admit, but it was a gut instinct, and I had to trust that I was being guided. I'm sure they'll love it. After all, he is still a member of that family, and I'm sure his love of country will continue throughout his lifetime whether he's the king or not."

"I have to admit the idea to open the house and have the decorations and music flowing through it in case the weather changes is genius. If everyone comes inside we may be able to find the party planner dressed to camouflage himself among the decorations!"

"Behave, Carter," Grace said with a serene smile. "I wasn't too sure when I met him—he was such a self-important, pompous, and arrogant man, but he was recommended by several people. I must say (personality aside), I'm very pleased with how he's coordinated everything."

The sound of an approaching car put an end to the conversation as they all jumped to rush to the windows to see if it was Nigel with their long-awaited guests. Courtney was the smallest and fastest of them.

"It's them!" she cried, dashing from the window into the hallway, with the rest of the family following hot on her heels. She flung open the large front door and hopped eagerly from foot to foot.

As a flushed Carrie stepped out of the car, she was instantly inundated by a sea of arms all trying to hug her at once. Only Grace stood back, allowing her offspring their usual exuberance, waiting patiently for her chance to greet her eldest daughter.

"Carrie, you look absolutely radiant, Darling," she told her as she finally got her opportunity to envelop her in a warm hug.

"Thank you. You look as beautiful as ever, Mom. So does everyone; oh, it's so good to see you all!" Carrie glanced around at the members of her large, sometimes rowdy family. "I can't believe we're here."

She turned to look over her shoulder and everyone's eyes followed her gaze, landing on Nigel and the man standing beside him. Chelsea took in the regal stature, the handsome face with the olive skin, the dark hair, and the intense brown eyes that never left Carrie for a second.

"Everyone, I'd like you to meet Antonio Dominguez." Carrie blushed at the words as she held out her hand for Antonio to step forward and join her among the sea of faces.

Chelsea watched the way he moved with interest. It was a mixture between arrogant and sensual; a cat-like grace combined with unashamed pride and barely restrained passion. How could so much be contained in a few steps?

She could see what Carrie saw in this man, physically at least. The jury was still out on the rest. He was standing there, his expression serious as Carrie giggled over something with Cassie.

"Bet she's not going to know what's hit her on her wedding night!" Courtney whispered in Chelsea's ear, causing her to choke down her laughter. Chelsea nudged her and shushed her, afraid Carrie or Antonio would hear. He briefly allowed a tiny smile to cross his face and Chelsea flushed, wondering if he had caught Courtney's outrageous comment. At that moment, his eyes caught hers, and she just knew he had overheard.

"Let's all go inside and sit down," Chelsea stammered before anyone noticed the awkward moment. Carter was already looking at her quizzically, wondering what was up with her all of a sudden.

They all made their way into the family room and sat, immediately bombarding Carrie with questions about the flight, her work, New York. She held up her hands in surrender.

"Slow down everyone," she laughed. "The flight was absolutely fine, New York is still as great as ever, and work is going well."

"How about you, Antonio, do you like the city?"

"I have to confess I haven't had much time to explore the city so far; I've only been there for about two weeks, as there was so much official business to complete before I left Spain. I was exhausted.

Carrie helped me by finding an apartment to rent, and mostly I've been busy unpacking and finding furniture. I must admit to feeling more at home here at the moment. The scenery reminds me of Spain, and your home is very beautiful. I particularly like the colors of the decorations."

Antonio smiled at Grace, a wide smile that transformed his serious face and lit up those dark, brooding eyes. Chelsea watched, bemused as even the ever-composed Grace Carpenter flushed slightly at the compliment…and the look.

"Oh, thank you, I'm so glad you like them, and I hope you will consider this your home and treat it as such."

"You are most kind, Mrs. Carpenter. For all the official welcomes I have had in my lifetime, I think perhaps this has been the warmest and the most pleasant.

"I have heard so much about you all, I feel as if I know you already. I am very honored that you are holding this party for us; I know Carrie feels the same."

"Don't be silly, as if we wouldn't! And please, call me Grace."

"Have you set a date for the big day yet?" Cassie interjected.

"Not yet," Carrie replied. "Antonio has only attended church in New York twice since he's just moved there, and was only baptized in January."

"Yes, I heard about this baptism. Tell me more—I might be able to use it in one of my stories."

"Trust you, Cassie, always looking for something to write about in everything. Don't be surprised, Antonio, if someone matching your description turns up in a romance novel in the near future. I'm sure I already recognize many of her characters," Carrie laughed.

"I am already the main character in a romance novel, one that is being written every second of every day," he said tenderly, reaching out to stroke Carrie's golden mane.

"Is it just me or did it just get really hot in here?" Courtney said with a cheeky grin, fanning herself dramatically.

Chelsea glowered at her, trying to keep Courtney in check before she made any more inappropriate remarks, but the effect was negated by her flaming cheeks still burning from the earlier embarrassment.

Courtney had quickly stepped behind Chelsea as she made the comment. She hoped Antonio didn't think it was her who made the quip. "Antonio, please tell us about your baptism. We'd all like to know the story!"

"Well, first of all, while Carrie was in my company as she was reporting the incident with the oil tanker, I had noticed some interesting traits in her, and one night I questioned her about them.

I had already fallen in love with her by then, and when I learned some of the beliefs she held, I was curious about her religion. I knew instantly those beliefs were a large part of what made Carrie the amazing woman she was, and I wanted to learn more, so I read everything I could get my hands on."

"And Carrie knew nothing of this?"

"No, at the time there were a million and one things that seemed to make a relationship with her impossible. I had a lot of soul searching and thinking to do.

"When she left me to return to America, I realized I didn't want to live without her, no matter what the cost, but I still couldn't see a way to make it work, even though we were communicating daily, often hourly at that time.

"I went to have a heartfelt talk with my priest, who told me to speak directly to God and listen to my heart for the answers. Well, I did, and the answers I received all led me to believe that Carrie was my destiny, the path I was supposed to walk.

"So I contacted the Mormon church's mission office in Madrid. I think they were quite surprised to hear from me, not only a Catholic, but the Prince of Spain. The sweet lady who answered the phone didn't believe it was really me.

"She scolded me with 'Elder Barker, you've got to stop calling here and playing jokes on us. We're very busy in the office right now working on transfers for next week.' He'd raised his voice to a falsetto to imitate the woman.

"It took all I could do to convince her I was telling the truth, that I was the Prince of Spain, and that I truly wanted to meet with someone who could teach me more about their religion."

By now everyone was laughing, Cassie and Courtney the loudest of all.

Chelsea grinned as she imagined that scenario. *I would have fainted dead away if I'd taken that call!*

Encouraged by their laughter, Antonio continued the story.

"Anyway, once they realized I was actually serious, they agreed to introduce me to a couple of Elders who could teach me, and arranged for them to visit me several times a week."

"Mom, you'll never guess who one of them was!" Carrie jumped in. "Kyle Anderson!"

"No! James and Carolyn's son?"

"Yep! I knew Kyle had been away on a mission, but I had no idea he was in Madrid; I'd have looked him up if I'd known."

"I didn't know either. It's a very small world sometimes, isn't it?"

"You bet, and he was due home just a couple of weeks before Antonio left Spain. I hope you don't mind, but I asked him to come to the party tonight.

"As you can guess, he's become a close friend of Antonio's now, and I thought it would be nice for him to know someone at the party…besides all of us, of course."

"Of course I don't mind! I hadn't heard Kyle was back or he would have certainly been included. His parents are already on the guest list. Antonio, forgive us for getting off track, please continue."

"Not at all, I'm delighted that Kyle will be here tonight. I owe him everything. He and his companion were very patient with me, explaining everything, answering all my questions—even the impertinent ones. And I had a *lot* of questions! His eyes opened wide to emphasize the fact, and they all laughed. He seemed to be enjoying having an audience.

"We explored how much my current religion meant to me, and he showed me how it could mean even more than ever before. He explained how Mormons believe there is good in every religion that brings people closer to Jesus Christ."

Chelsea leaned forward, her chin resting in the palm of her left hand, eyes glued on Antonio as he continued.

"By the end of the third week, the Spirit had witnessed to me that Jesus Christ lives, that He is our Savior, and atoned for our sins in a way I had never felt or understood before. I learned this fact in my childhood, but now that knowledge had made its way from my head to my heart. I had my own testimony that it was true.

"Through almost constant study and prayer while Carrie and I were separated I was sure this was the church for me. I knew I was not joining it just to be with Carrie, but through true faith in Jesus Christ and gratitude for His atoning sacrifice."

Peace settled on his face as he squeezed Carrie's hand, looking lovingly into her eyes.

Chelsea sat enthralled as once again God was demonstrating the power of His love, the way He mapped out a path for them all, sometimes filled with adversity, but always showing them the way to overcome and find peace and happiness within His great plan.

Even cynical Courtney had a hand on her heart and a soft expression on her elfin features. Cassie, of course, was still taking notes on her mental computer to transcribe when she got back to her office.

"By the time I was absolutely certain I wished to be baptized into a new faith, I then had to find a solution to the other problem: abdicating the throne of Spain. My priest had also advised me not to handle this problem alone but to talk with my father and together we could find a solution.

"So I did exactly that. With my father's help, we figured out a way for me to perhaps be able to step down from my responsibilities without it costing my country too much."

"But what about your mother, the queen?" interrupted Cassie, eager to get all the gory details. "Surely she wasn't happy about all this."

"Ah, yes. My mother! You probably know that by this time she had approached Carrie - without my knowledge of course - warning her to stay away from me or she could damage my reputation and, as a result, damage Spain and the monarchy.

"Although my mother was wrong to do so, it all seemed almost justified when the newspapers went wild with photos of my indiscreet glances at Carrie at my sister's engagement announcement."

"Yes, we all saw the unfortunate articles that ran," Grace murmured.

"I apologize sincerely for any distress it may have caused your family. Carrie already knows how sorry I am and has forgiven me. I am hoping you all can do the same."

Antonio bowed his head, looking truly remorseful for Carrie being thrust into the limelight in such a horrible way.

"There is nothing to forgive as far as I'm concerned, Antonio. What I see in my daughter is great happiness and a wonderful future ahead of her," Grace replied.

"Seconded," Chelsea agreed quickly.

"Thirded," Carter added.

"Fourthed," Cassie jumped in, pumping a fist high in the air.

"Honestly, you two, there are no such words. Carter, you're only an architect, so I can forgive you. But Cassie, you're supposed to be a writer!" Courtney rolled her eyes at them.

"Yes, I'm a writer, so I can make up words where I want. It's called 'artistic license,'" Cassie argued. The group burst into laughter, and the tense moment passed.

"So why the public declaration and engagement?" Chelsea pressed, wanting to hear the ending of the fairytale story.

Antonio grinned at Carrie. "After my mother's warning, Carrie wouldn't speak to me. She did exactly as my mother instructed. She ignored my emails and texts, wouldn't answer or return my calls. Nothing.

"I was in agony! A credit to Carrie, she followed my mother's instructions. To. The. Letter.

"She even wrote a wonderful article professing her love for me and explaining how it occurred, which quieted the press completely.

"Calling a press conference and sending her boss an invitation for his newspaper to be represented, specifically naming her on the invitation, was the only way I could think of to get her to go to Madrid.

"And addressing her publicly was the only way to get her to listen."

Carrie gasped. "Antonio, you never told me that! You did all that just to get my attention?"

"You never asked, so I never told," he smiled at her.

"After I had decided that course of action, I also thought it would be a good time to appeal to the people on behalf of my sister, to ensure they would accept her as the new heir apparent. The Spanish are very passionate, and few can resist a good love story.

"I just knew it would all work out; it was as if everything fell into place as soon as I understood everything Elder Anderson was teaching me. The Lord worked miracles for us, and the rest, as they say, is history.

"Carrie agreed to be my wife, which I guess you all saw on television multiple times, and she attended my baptism later that afternoon. It was Elder Anderson who baptized me.

I would have been baptized even if Carrie had refused me, which was all the confirmation I needed to realize I was truly doing this for the right reasons. So now here we are."

Antonio had put his arm around Carrie when he asked the family for their forgiveness; now he lifted her fingers to his lips and kissed them gently.

Chelsea's heart lurched; it was something Clark used to do in their tender moments. She was glad when Courtney broke the spell between the two by asking another question.

"So, is there anything at all you're struggling with, being a Mormon I mean?"

Antonio nodded slowly. "As a matter of fact there is, only one. Giving up coffee! It's practically the staple diet of Spaniards."

"Well, if you're in need of a fix, come to me. I've got a secret stash," Courtney joked.

"Courtney Carpenter, don't encourage him! It's something we're working on together, and he's doing really well. Don't make him relapse!" scolded Carrie, putting on her best Army Sergeant act.

Chelsea couldn't help but join in with the laughter. She had a feeling she was going to like Antonio, and he was obviously head-over-heels in love with Carrie.

No one could doubt his devotion after everything he had sacrificed. She had never seen Carrie more carefree and happy.

She was so pleased her sister had found her prince and was living her very own fairytale.

CHAPTER FOUR

Chelsea was glad to be home. The party had been amazing, as had the rest of the vacation. Antonio fit right in with the family as if he'd always been part of it and had been welcomed with open arms at church.

His reunion with Kyle Anderson had been an emotional one, and the bond between the two men was plain to see. They had so obviously become close friends during Antonio's lessons, and Kyle's success as a missionary was pretty legendary. After all, how many chances do missionaries get to baptize a prince?

The only blip on the weekend had been Courtney's usual refusal to attend church with the family, although she had hesitated before answering in the negative this time, which was a first.

Chelsea wasn't sure what to make of the hesitation; she normally flat-out refused straight away. No matter, Courtney was who she was, and they loved her no matter what. She added a special spice to the family, and they would always support her freedom to choose. After all, free agency was also a tenet of the Mormon faith.

Courtney had been raised differently than the others for the first seven years of her life and had suffered a lot by the time she came into their family. It was understandable that she had wavered between being angry with God for her fate—especially the death of her mother—and denying His existence entirely.

Over the years they had come to respect each other's way of life, simply hoping that Courtney would follow by example. Now any comments made were good-natured teasing, all done in fun.

As far as Chelsea could tell, apart from not attending church and drinking coffee, Courtney actually lived naturally by the same code of ethics and morals that the rest of the family did. She was a good person, kind and caring, if a little impetuous and free-spirited.

They'd all long since decided to let Courtney be Courtney, but Sunday's hesitation still intrigued Chelsea. Perhaps it was Antonio's conversion that had sparked an interest. She thought it was a shame Carrie and Antonio had returned to New York; an outside influence might have been successful in influencing Courtney where the family had failed.

Shaking her head and taking a deep breath, as if to call herself back to reality, Chelsea put the matter out of her mind. For now, she herself needed to get back into the frame of mind for work.

Not only did she find a great manuscript among the pile that she took with her when she left the office for the short vacation, but the board was meeting to look over the résumés that had been submitted in their absence along with the recommendations of the headhunter.

They had voted early in the morning the previous Friday, with the majority being in favor of Grace's idea to create a new position. The recruitment drive was implemented immediately, just as Grace and Charles had planned.

Chelsea unpacked her bags slowly, relieved to be back in her sanctuary. She had a great time, but there were many moments that made it difficult to cope. The speeches made at the party brought every memory of her own engagement party rushing back in Technicolor.

Unlike the recently-baptized Antonio, Clark had been a member of the church all his life, and they wouldn't have had to wait for a year before they could be married in the temple.

They had been planning a short engagement, eager to begin their lives as husband and wife. He had a six-month tour of duty to complete, beginning two days after the engagement party, and the wedding was being planned for just two weeks after his return.

She would never forget the moment she heard the news. She was actually at home, poring over bridal magazines with her mom, Courtney, Cassie, and Maggie,

They were throwing around ideas and searching for inspiration to make it the most magical day of her life. She could remember clearly the dress they were gushing over on the glossy page, but the weeks afterward were almost a complete blank.

She remembered her mom's arms around her as she collapsed. There was an awful noise, a low pitched, guttural wailing that she would later learn was coming from her own mouth. After that…nothing.

The next firm memory she had was viewing this condo with the real estate agent and shutting herself away from the world after signing on the dotted line. From there, she had rebuilt her life one tiny baby step at a time, praying to God to give her the strength to carry on without Clark.

Her first outing was venturing back to church. In those early days, she arranged for someone to drop off work to her at home, and then she immersed herself in it, returning the completed tasks to the office in exchange for more work. This continued until she was finally emotionally ready to make an appearance at the office.

It had been a slow process, but she had taken so much comfort and inspiration from her mom, who had handled the same thing with far more strength than she had thought possible, and from God, who had never left her side during the bleakest times, even when she didn't attend church. He saw her through.

She didn't question the reason Clark had been taken from her. He'd answered a calling by joining the army; that had been his path to follow, and she had chosen to join him and support him on that path, knowing the risks.

She still had many blessings; she had her family, she had her work with the youth group at church, she had her job at the family business, and she had her faith.

She also had the perfect example of His magnificent creations right outside her windows, reminding her each day of His greatness. It was more than enough.

—∞∞∞—

"Suzanna Birkenstoff," Grace called out. "Kade Richardson and Jamie Sutherland. Are we agreed that those are the ones we want on the shortlist for interviews from the applicants so far?"

Charles and Chelsea added their agreement. They'd had applications flooding in to the headhunter, but these three stood out above the others.

Chelsea knew they couldn't possibly interview everyone who applied and that they had to narrow them down, but she felt sad for the ones whose applications were gathered up in a stack to receive the thanks-but-no-thanks letters.

It hadn't been done lightly; it had taken the three of them nearly five hours to go through the applications already received, and the headhunter had only been working on it since last Friday. It was likely they would probably receive hundreds more over the next week or so.

"Charles, can you compile an interview schedule starting next week, maybe making up varied teams of four? I'd like to include myself, someone else in a managerial role, one current marketing department head, and the fourth to represent a cross-section of people throughout the firm.

We want to interview a maximum of fifteen to twenty if there are that many with the correct qualifications, and from what we've seen so far, I think there will be. The interviews need to be quite in-depth, so splitting the task makes sense.

That way no one has to spend all of their precious time over the next few weeks interviewing except me, and I'm sure I can be spared. You can handle things if I'm tied up?"

Charles nodded his agreement and said he would get right on it.

"Great, so include these three candidates to start with, then we'll see who else we have recommended to us. We want to give ourselves the best possible shot of finding exactly the right person; it's not just about qualifications, as we all know.

Depending on how far they have to travel, it's going to be a bit of a juggling process, but I'm sure we'll pull it all together as always. Any questions?"

No one had anything to ask or add, so Grace wrapped up the meeting. Chelsea rose to leave the conference room and head back to her office. She was surprised to find a smiling Carter sitting on the edge of Beth's desk.

"I hope you aren't distracting Beth from her work," she said, a stern expression on her face, hands on hips.

"Actually, I was trying to arrange a dinner date, but I'm getting knocked back," Carter said, shaking his head and sighing. Beth giggled demurely and Chelsea smiled inside while keeping her pretend annoyance on her face.

"What are you doing here anyway? I thought you were leaving this morning."

"I was supposed to, but I checked in with the big boss last night and he told me I may as well stay through the weekend. My client is still considering the plans I drew up for their new branch building; some internal argument is going on between the brothers and they can't decide which way to use the internal space.

So until that's settled, the project is on hold. Just thought I'd see if some of my favorite girls could come to lunch. Mom said she's too busy, Courtney is holed up in her office and won't answer anyone, and Beth has already knocked me back for dinner, so I don't suppose lunch with her is in the cards either. So that leaves you."

"I see, so I was Plan B. The backup plan."

"Yep, scraping the bottom of the barrel, but there you have it. You coming?"

Chelsea glanced at her watch; it was just after noon, a little early for her to be taking her lunch break, but she figured she could be flexible just this once. "Do I have any meetings I need to be back for this afternoon, Beth?"

"Just the one at 3 with that new author you wanted to chat with. Handy that he's a local and you get to meet him in person for a change."

"Right. I'll be sure I'm back in plenty of time for that. I wouldn't want to spend that much time with Carter anyway."

"Hey!" Carter laughed. "I guess that was payback. Come on, I'm starving."

"You're always hungry. Do you ever think of anything else but your stomach?" Chelsea asked as they headed out the door.

"Hmm, sometimes," Carter replied, with a puppy dog look back in Beth's direction.

Chelsea cuffed him over the back of the head. "Get a move on; I haven't got all day."

Sitting across from each other in the restaurant at The Homestead, Chelsea and Carter passed a pleasant hour chatting about their work, family, and his life in San Francisco.

It sounded like a fascinating place, and Chelsea wondered if she could visit someday. She didn't like to be away from work for too long; she felt adrift without it to anchor her.

She didn't know if she would always feel that way, but for now she needed that anchor and the demands of the heavy workload that showed no signs of letting up. *I'll get to San Francisco someday, just not any time soon.*

"You look sad all of a sudden," Carter noted.

"Not at all, I'm fine."

Chelsea smiled at her brother, brushing her feelings off as she always did. She hated when they worried about her or fussed over her. She did her best to hide anything negative going on inside. Everybody had enough to deal with in their own lives without adding her troubles to their plates.

"I want to ask you something, but it's a bit sensitive and I'm not too sure how to bring it up."

"Look, if you genuinely want to ask Beth out, it's okay by me. I was only teasing before. But would it be fair, considering you live so far away and will be gone soon?"

"It's not that," Carter shook his head. "It's not about me; it's about you."

Uh oh, Chelsea thought. *This probably can't be going anywhere good.*

"Okay then."

She started to rip apart a leftover bread roll, busying her hands as she waited for her brother to pluck up the courage to say what he needed to say. She heard Carter take a deep breath, and kept her head down, eyes on the mess she was making on her plate.

"The morning that Carrie arrived with Antonio, I saw you blushing and looking all coy at Antonio, and I saw you exchange a…look, if you know what I mean. What was that about? I hope you're not developing a crush on him, Chelsea, because I don't want to see you hurt again."

The words had come out in a rush, as if he was frightened of her reaction or perhaps of hearing the answer. Chelsea's hands stopped their desecration of the innocent roll, and she raised her head to stare at her brother, mouth open in shock. The expression on Carter's face was so serious, so stern, yet pitying.

Chelsea couldn't help herself; she burst out laughing. Soon she was in a helpless fit of giggles, tears streaming down her face as she gasped for air.

"What? What is it?"

Carter was frantic, but Chelsea could barely breathe for laughing, let alone answer him. Courtney's comment that day, Carter's face right now, and his ridiculous interpretation of what had transpired in that moment all combined to give her the best laugh she'd had in ages.

By the time it had subsided to hiccups and quiet giggles, she felt weak all over.

She knew she was acting like a child, but it was all just so...*funny*, and it was a wonderful release to be so helpless with laughter, to be completely out of control. It had been a long time since she'd felt that way.

Normally, she kept all her emotions carefully in check, reined in and under lock and key, buried as deep inside her as she could possibly hide them.

Carter had caused a breach, but at least it was a good one. A really funny one!

"You silly goose," she finally managed to say. "Have you been worrying about that all this time?"

"If I'm being so silly, then tell me what was happening." He just wasn't seeing the humor in his question.

Chelsea rubbed the last of the tears from her eyes. "I blushed because of something Courtney said." She giggled again as she recalled the comment. "And I glanced up at Antonio to see if he had heard. This tiny smile crossed his face and then he looked up, just as Courtney hid behind me. He caught my eye and I knew he had heard it, and probably thought it was me, which caused me to blush even more."

"Yes, and stammer like a schoolgirl. You can see why I thought what I did."

"I suppose so, yes, but you should have asked me about it sooner."

"I should have, you're right," Carter smiled, the relief obvious in his eyes. "So what did our darling baby sister say to cause you to blush?"

"I'm not sure if I can repeat it!"

"Oh, go on, it's only us. Don't you think I deserve to know, after all the anguish you put me through."

Chelsea rested her fist under her chin with her forefinger tapping on her lips to pretend deliberate consideration of his point, and then nodded in agreement. She leaned in close and he followed her lead. Their heads were almost touching as she said to him in a stage whisper, "I bet she won't know what's hit her on her wedding night."

Carter threw back his head and roared with laughter. "Oh my gosh! Only Courtney could meet a royal for the first time and come out with something like that. Are you certain he heard?"

"Absolutely."

"No wonder you were all atwitter then. How embarrassing! I'm sorry I picked it up all wrong, but you have to admit how it looked, considering I didn't see Courtney whisper to you."

"I forgive you," Chelsea grinned. "I can imagine how it looked. I hope no one else interpreted it the same way though."

"I don't think anyone else noticed. You're probably safe enough."

"Thanks for the laugh anyway, Carter. I guess I should be getting back to work."

Carter settled the bill and they headed for his car.

"You know, being my twin," Chelsea commented as they strolled across the parking lot, "you should know me better than that. Aren't you supposed to be able to tell what I'm feeling?"

"I do, Chelsea, much more often than you think," he replied quietly, wrapping an arm around her shoulder in a brotherly hug.

CHAPTER FIVE

Grace, Chelsea, Lisa (the head of marketing for the children's section), and James (a member of Chelsea's editing team) made up the interview panel for the day.

They had conducted two interviews so far, and had another two candidates yet to see. As Chelsea had suspected, the lure of a position within such a well-known, multi-branched firm had attracted applicants from all over.

Grace had been worried that the very fact the position was in the head office in Utah would prevent some of the best talent from applying. Although it was a state-renowned for its intense natural beauty, winter sports, and wealth of national parks, it wasn't considered one of the most exciting places to live full-time.

When people relocated, they normally wanted to head to the larger, more famous cities for the experience and the opportunities. Working for Carpenter Global Press had been enough to counteract that, and applications had come from as far away as Great Britain and even Malaysia.

One of the candidates had been ruled out immediately; his first answer had explained how he wanted to broaden the company's repertoire and introduce many more book categories such as graphic horror and female erotica.

Not only was his arrogance off-putting, but he hadn't done his research. This was a family business, one that reflected their family values. They steered clear of intense violence, anything pornographic, genres they considered trashy. They would never publish books with a thin plot, characters that were two-dimensional, or a story written just as an excuse to include lots of sex scenes.

Everybody employed by the firm understood the criteria and accepted working within it. Courtney, of course, pushed those boundaries further than anyone else dared, often fighting for a book that Grace would have instantly dismissed.

However, they all had a feeling that this particular candidate had no understanding at all of the firm's foundation or what it tried to achieve. They were able to scratch him off the list without hesitation.

Chelsea had instantly taken to another candidate, Suzanna, and had given her high scores on many aspects. She was a mother of two teenage daughters and she kept a close eye on their reading matter.

She was a huge fan of the firm and its code of ethics, as well as its unique rating system that had been introduced by Courtney as a way of identifying for all their customers any books that may contain themes less suitable for their youngest readers.

Suzanna would fit in perfectly here. She was local and didn't need to move and uproot her children. Her skillset was good. However, her marketing experience was limited to a much smaller company. That was a bit of a concern, especially when heading up a large and already established expert team.

They perused the résumé of the next candidate, due to be shown into the boardroom within a few moments.

"Up next is Kade Richardson, 29 years old and already head of marketing at…where was it, oh yes, Bostonian Books. Anyone know the firm?" Grace asked.

"I do," Chelsea said. "They're a big firm but quite a niche market. They specialize in historical novels. They include fiction, historical romances, and mysteries, but what they are really about are autobiographies and biographies—the stories of actual lives. Everything from famous politicians to kitchen maids or anyone who felt they had a story to tell.

Clark was a big fan; we…I mean *I,* have several of their publications at home, especially the ones by Vietnam veterans."

"Okay, so he'll be used to working very closely with the editors from a marketing stance, coaxing them to get exactly what he needs from people who are essentially non-authors, maybe even working with ghost writers. That's interesting; a useful skillset, don't you think, Chelsea?"

Chelsea knew her mother was trying to deliberately force her to move on, pulling her mind away from memories of Clark and making her focus on the matter at hand.

"Absolutely. These are one-off, unique experiences. And no disrespect to the authors, but they're not very well-written, rough manuscripts to start. To work so closely with a team to turn them into the perfectly-produced, massive sellers that BB releases shows not only a deep understanding of his market, but also a great sensitivity to the projects themselves.

I'm quite excited about this one; if he lives up to our expectations, he's going to be absolutely perfect."

A knock on the door prevented any more discussion as Grace's assistant popped her head round and asked if they were ready for the next candidate. All eyes were on the door as the strong and promising applicant stepped into the boardroom. Chelsea sucked in a breath as he strode toward the table.

He was tall, just over six feet, broad-shouldered and slim-hipped, dressed in a well-cut charcoal grey suit with a light grey silk tie over a pristine white shirt. Chelsea felt her heart flutter as she took in the vision standing before her.

Wow, he's all male, she thought, shocked at her own reaction. She hadn't reacted to man like this since Clark, but she had never seen one to compare to him, not in her way of thinking anyway.

She pulled herself from her wayward thoughts as she realized he was holding his hand out for her to shake, having made his way down the panel of interviewers. She half stood and took it, feeling a jolt shoot through her as he wrapped her small hand in his large, masculine one.

His handshake was firm but gentle, and when he smiled and introduced himself, his face lost that dark, brooding expression, lightening into something that could have been a divine piece of art.

Stop it, Chelsea! she told herself firmly. *He's just a man, and beauty on the outside is superficial and unimportant. You know better than to be taken in by it.*

"Thank you for your application and interest in working for the firm, Mr. Richardson," Grace began. "Please take a seat and we can begin the interview."

Chelsea watched, enthralled as the tall man folded himself gracefully into the chair. He had dark brown, thick, luxurious hair that was cut short at the back and sides, but kept a touch long on top, perfectly groomed and styled.

It begged for fingers to be run through it, tousling the perfect look. He was relaxed and at ease despite the imposing panel of four waiting to interrogate him.

"Would you please tell us a little about your current position?"

As Kade spoke about his responsibilities and aims in his current job, Chelsea was surprised to see such warmth and sensitivity shining in those eyes; she didn't think it was possible with that color.

He was beginning to make her think of a sled dog, those blue eyes cold and aloof, almost frightening with their intensity. But the creature itself was warm and loving, hardworking and loyal to its last breath.

Oh my goodness, what am I doing? I'm comparing a job applicant to an animal!

She was letting her mind wander to the most ridiculous of places. What was the matter with her? She tried to regain her train of thought, concentrate on his words instead of watching that masculine jaw move as he spoke, but she was almost hypnotized. She felt like she was drowning, struggling to reach the water's surface.

Sexual attraction to her fiancé had been hard to overcome, especially once they were promised to each other, and that was understandable. This reaction to a complete stranger was not.

She should be able to look at him as she would her view from her deck, appreciative of the beauty of one of God's creations and awed by the wonder of it, but nothing more. Absolutely nothing more!

"Tell me why you want to work for Carpenter Global Press when you are obviously so attached and invested in your current firm."

Chelsea realized Grace was talking again. She wondered how much of the interview she had already missed and gave herself a mental dressing down for her failing. Her work was everything to her now, and this was an important moment for the company; she couldn't afford to be anything less than fully invested in the process.

She kept her eyes averted, staring at the copy of the résumé and scribbling in her notepad, which allowed her to listen properly to his answers.

"It's true I love working for Bostonian Books, but working for Carpenter Global Press has been a dream of mine. Not only is the firm large and progressive, allowing plenty of opportunity to learn and to grow within it, but I am full of admiration for what Mr. John Carpenter accomplished here.

"Rarely does one come across an entrepreneur whose idea of success is not based simply on making money, but of trying to accomplish some good in the world, standing up for what he believed in, and making those beliefs clear to everyone involved.

"He took a business idea and used it to guide and advise others. He wanted to set an example for people to be even better, to strive to be the best they could be in every area of their lives, demonstrating love and respect for their fellow man, showing compassion and understanding when they or others fail or falter.

"It's what I believe the man stood for, and I was glad to see that the company today still holds true to its original values and follows his vision. I would be honored to be part of that."

"How about relocating from Boston to the head office here in Utah? How do you feel about that?"

Chelsea heard the slight tremor in her mom's voice and looked over at her sharply. Her face was pinched and her eyes too glassy. Chelsea was instantly furious with this candidate. How dare he come in here with his pretty speeches and upset her mom by talking about her father!

So he had done his research to be able to answer the questions, but he had it all too down pat. If it seemed too good to be true, it probably was. She kept her eyes down as he answered.

"I've traveled quite extensively in my life, but I was born and raised in Salt Lake City, so I'm almost a local. From ages 19 to 21 I was a missionary serving in the West Indies Mission where I got to work in French Guiana and on the islands of Guadalupe and St. Martin.

"From there, I graduated from BYU and went on to the Wharton School, where I completed my MBA. Then I moved to Boston where I'd already secured the position at Bostonian Books.

"There comes a time in life when a man needs to decide where he wants to call home. I've reached that stage and given it careful consideration, and home for me will always be back in Utah. I would love to relocate here, make it a permanent move, and be able to call it home again. My mother would be thrilled to have her wandering son back home."

Chelsea scribbled angrily on her pad, looking at the notes she had written. Local boy, Mormon, understands and admires company values, graduated from one of best business schools in the country.

Oh yes, it was definitely all too good to be true—he must be an expert in public relations to come out with all that, having only been asked two questions so far.

She was glad when the interview moved on to the more technical aspects, delving into the marketing skills he claimed to have and away from the personal aspects of the man.

After Kade left, Chelsea straightened her back and rubbed her neck, which had grown stiff from being deliberately bent over her pad for the duration of the interview. She stared moodily at the detailed assessment questionnaire she was required to fill in.

Since the makeup of the interview panels would change, it was necessary for them all to provide their thoughts on each applicant they saw. This would allow Grace to give due consideration to each of their opinions on each candidate. Chelsea couldn't seem to find fault with his qualifications.

He hadn't been fazed by anything they had thrown at him and had shown a deep understanding and knowledge of his chosen profession, as well as answering without hesitation how he felt he could make the position work with the existing structure within the firm.

That was exactly the problem, the main stumbling block for Chelsea. It all seemed too smooth, too perfect. She filled in the form then added a note in large uppercase letters in the box provided for additional information:

TOO PERFECT. UNSURE IF HE IS TO BE TRUSTED, BACKGROUND CHECK REQUIRED ON ALL DETAILS AND ANSWERS GIVEN.

She stared at the sheet, wondering if her comment looked childish and petulant, and inwardly examining her reasons for writing it.

Could it just be because she was angry with herself for finding him attractive? No, she wasn't that unprofessional. She admitted she was angry with him for upsetting her mom by bringing up her father, but it wasn't just that either.

She decided her comment should stand, just in case he had merely done some background checks of his own and spouted off what he knew they wanted to hear. If he did turn out to be genuine, then fine, he had nothing to worry about and no harm, no foul.

There was just something about him that set her alarm bells ringing, and she couldn't ignore that; it needed to be followed up on and investigated.

They would be interviewing for at least another week yet, so there was plenty of time to gather the information she had requested before a final decision had to be made. Finishing the form, she added it to the pile of others and picked up the folder for the next applicant.

CHAPTER SIX

It was nearly three weeks later when Chelsea ran into Grace in the parking lot as they both arrived for work.

"Good morning, Chelsea. How are you this morning?"

"Doing great. How about you, Grace?" Chelsea referred to her mother by her given name in their professional setting; 'Mom' was saved for their personal times.

"I'd like to stop by your office this morning and discuss something. Will you be available?" Grace said.

"Of course. I'm always available for you."

About 9 a.m. Beth buzzed Chelsea and informed her that Mrs. Carpenter was there to see her. Chelsea smiled and told Beth to send her through.

Having lost track of time, she hurried to clear the untidy pile of unsorted manuscripts from the spare chair on the opposite side of her desk. She dumped them on the floor next to the shelves, promising herself that she would get around to them later that day.

"Hi, Grace! Glad to see you down in the lower echelon today," she teased. "What's up?"

Grace smiled. "I want to talk to you about several things actually, Dear."

"Uh oh, that sounds ominous. You'd better take a seat." Chelsea motioned to the sitting area in the corner of the room and took the loveseat across from her mom.

Grace settled comfortably into the chair. "I asked Beth to get us some hot chocolate on my way in. It's midmorning after all; isn't that usually a break time?"

"Great!" was all Chelsea added, laughing. Having a hot drink meant this was going to take a while. Something was up and she was curious about the nature of the visit, but she knew Grace wouldn't explain until Beth had delivered the tray and ensured their privacy.

Beth knocked gently on the door to announce her entrance. "Cookies as well! Gosh, we are splurging today. Thanks, Beth. I'll have to park out by the entrance to the tram tonight and jog up the mountain to my condo to work this off!"

Chelsea never indulged in hot chocolate at work but would never offend her mother by refusing it. She obviously had something on her mind and wanted them to have the comfort food to keep the discussion comfortable.

"Thank you," Grace called as Beth retreated and closed the door.

"Come on then, spill it! I'm dying to know why I have the pleasure of your company this morning, not to mention the treats," Chelsea said, picking up one of Mrs. Field's best chocolate chip cookies and nibbling on the edge.

Grace had been a friend of the founder of Mrs. Field's Cookies after the Fields moved their business to Park City and, although the company had been sold to investors, Grace and Debbi Field had remained great friends, working on a number of philanthropic community service projects together.

Debbi had been a real source of comfort to Grace at the time of John's accident on the slopes above Park City, and Carpenter Global continued to have fresh Mrs. Field's cookies available in the company snack room.

"First, I wanted to tell you about an idea Courtney has come up with and see if you think it's worth pursuing or just another of her hare-brained schemes."

"This should be good," Chelsea replied with a grin, settling back in her chair with a cookie to enjoy hearing about her little sister's latest brainstorm.

"You know how Antonio has to rethink a career now that he is no longer in politics?"

"No longer in politics is a bit of an understatement, Grace, but I get the point, yes."

"Courtney suggested that we might recruit him into the family business. Carrie mentioned to her that he used to write all the family speeches and things himself, and while it's very different from fiction, she wondered if perhaps he might be a half-decent writer.

"She came up with the plan that he could collaborate with Cassie to do a series of romance novels based around a royal court, either historical or modern day. He would have the insider knowledge to share and it would give us a chance to see if he could actually have a career as an author on his own—a chance to evaluate his skills, so to speak."

"You know what? That's not half bad. My main concern would be his English; since it's a second language for him, it's very correct, quite stilted sometimes. I'm not sure how well that would read, unless you were possibly going for a British market."

"Yes, I think that's why she thought of the collaboration. Cassie could help him out with that, and by the time he was left to write on his own, he'd probably be more, um, integrated."

"You mean more American!"

"I suppose. I just wasn't sure if I should say it out loud."

"We're only talking about his speech patterns and ability to write for our market, so I think it's okay," Chelsea grinned at her mom.

"So you're in favor of the idea?"

"I am. What does everyone else think?"

"Courtney came to me first; we haven't spoken to anyone else yet. I just wanted to run it by you in case we were being ridiculous. You know once she puts her mind to it she can browbeat me into just about anything."

The women laughed together, knowing that the tiny Courtney was a true force to be reckoned with when she was passionate about something.

"True, but I really do think she might be onto a winner here. I could speak to Cassie and see what she thinks of the idea, but I'm sure she'll love it. Can you imagine what she'll make of having an actual prince advise her? She's going to be beside herself with excitement."

"I think so too. Maybe we should speak to Carrie and Antonio next, save getting Cassie's hopes up if they don't go for it."

Now that the course of action had been decided, both women relaxed to relish the first sips of their warm, soothing drinks.

"This is sheer decadence in the middle of the day; it's not even the middle of winter. I'm sure you didn't need to sweeten me up to talk to me about Courtney's idea."

"No, I didn't, but I thought you might need it when we discussed this next item." Chelsea straightened in her seat, anxious to learn the *real* reason Grace had asked to see her.

Grace opened the briefcase that never left her side and laid it on the table between them. She removed Chelsea's assessment form from Kade Richardson's interview. It was easy for Chelsea to see the big, bold letters she'd written weeks earlier. *Oh, so this is what it's all about.*

"I see from your notes you had some concerns over this particular applicant. Would you care to explain them more fully to me?"

"I don't know if I can," Chelsea frowned. "I struggled to put it into words for myself even. It's just that everything he said seemed to be the exact words we wanted to hear, someone who truly understood what this firm is all about, someone who shared our values, morals, and ethics.

"Add that to his seemingly impeccable education and experience, and his little speech about coming home…it put me on high alert. Nobody is perfect, but that's how he came across, and it made me wonder if it was all fake or if there was something he was hiding."

Grace nodded. "Okay, I think I understand what you're trying to say. You had an instinct and you were right to follow up on it. The only problem is, everything checks out.

"His family has been members of the church for generations, and he was born and raised in Salt Lake City, with a great recommendation from his bishop in Boston. He served his mission exactly where he said he did, and all his educational information is correct. I can't remember if he mentioned that he graduated *magna cum laude.*

"He even comes with a letter of recommendation from Boston Books, his current employer, that states they would be devastated to lose him but understand his desire to return to his home state and settle down. It says he will be a real asset to Carpenter Global."

Chelsea sighed. "I'm sorry, I must have been wrong then. I have no idea where the feeling of mistrust came from. I only knew that I felt like I wanted to keep my distance from him. Where did you get all that information?"

"I have my sources," Grace said, arching an eyebrow at her daughter. "The thing is, now that all the interviews are complete and the applications fully assessed, Kade Richardson really is the best candidate.

"He would be an excellent addition to the firm and I want to offer him the position today. I needed to know if you were agreeable to that, or if it was going to cause us a problem."

"No, no problem at all. I'll support your decision as always. Whatever I felt that day, I'll just have to forget it and start fresh. It was obviously unfounded."

"I knew you'd understand and take the professional view. Now tell me what's going on with you while we finish our chocolate. I, for one, am going to indulge in one more cookie."

A few weeks later Chelsea sat at her desk, engrossed in a manuscript. The intercom buzzed, interrupting her from her final proofing. She ignored it for a second; she was on the last page.

She didn't raise her eyes from the paper but instinctively held up a finger to indicate she needed a second, despite there being no one around to see her. Getting to the end of the lines of text, she breathed a sigh of relief and turned the page over. *Another deadline met well in advance,* she commended herself.

Work had been going particularly well recently. Her new author was perfect for the firm, and the unsolicited manuscript she had found among the pile had been easily approved after her recommendation.

Many of their regular clients had finished their first novels of the year, and getting them ready for summer release was proving to be an absolute joy. She was more than content that all was well in her life right now.

A second buzz brought a flush to her cheeks. She had been so busy mulling over how well work was going, she had completely forgotten about Beth waiting for a reply in the outer office.

"Sorry, what's up?"

"Kade Richardson is here and wondering if you can spare a few moments."

Chelsea's face darkened; so much for her perfect day. "Fine, I'll be right out."

She slipped through a small gap in the door, keeping her inner office obscured from view, feeling the need to guard it from the intruder. She saw him standing there, chatting casually with Beth as if he hadn't a care in the world.

Beth and Kade were so engrossed in conversation, they didn't notice Chelsea as she stepped from her office; both looked around when she cleared her throat.

Once again, her heart seemed to falter and stumble from its normal rhythm as she caught sight of his handsome face and dramatic 'Dan Stevens' eyes.

She rarely watched television at night, but at Beth's suggestion *Downton Abbey* had become a weekly addiction. She had never heard of Dan Stevens before that show, and didn't realize anyone else shared those captivating blue eyes.

She shook her head in frustration at allowing the distraction, bringing herself back to reality. Putting it down to her initial wariness of him, she stopped a few feet from him.

"Hello, what can I do for you?" she asked in the politest tone she could summon, putting out her hand toward him.

He took her hand in a firm handshake. "Hello, I remember now we were introduced during the interview. I'm just doing the rounds really, putting a face to all the names on the company phone roster and trying to find my way around, getting to know people. I just thought it would be polite to introduce myself to everyone."

"That's quite a tall order—it's a large firm."

"Indeed it is," he laughed, ignoring her curt manner. "I'll get there eventually though. I've met all the marketing teams and am working my way through the chief editors. You were on my list, so here I am."

"So I see. Well, since we've already met and you'd already seen my face and can now match it with the name, will that be all?"

"I guess so; it's not one I'm likely to forget in a hurry."

"No, Carpenter should be simple enough for you, considering it's in the name of the company that employs you."

"Actually, I was talking about your face."

Chelsea stared at him, stunned. Before she said something she might later regret, she whirled on her heel and stomped into her office, slamming the door behind her. She leaned against it, trying to calm her temper.

What kind of comment was that to make? We might be about equal in position in our day jobs, but I'm also a member of the board of directors and a Carpenter, and he would be well-advised not to forget it!

She let the door support her as she tried to calm her nerves.

A tentative knock came from the other side of the door. "Chelsea, its only Beth, can I come in?"

Chelsea stood, removing her weight from the back of the door and slowly opening it, peering over Beth's shoulder to ensure Kade had gone. Satisfied, she pulled the door open further and allowed her assistant to enter.

"I just wanted to make sure you were okay. I haven't seen you act that way since I first started here."

Chelsea bristled. "What way, exactly?" She tried to sound nonchalant as she walked toward her desk.

"Well…to be honest, impolite, rude, curt, whatever way you want to describe it really." The two were becoming more like friends than co-workers every day they worked together.

Chelsea slumped down into her chair. It must have taken Beth a lot of guts to say that to her, and it was probably born of real concern for her. "Was I really that bad?"

"Umm…yes, I'm afraid you were."

Chelsea waved Beth into the seat across from her desk. "Oh."

"Oh? That's all you're going to say. What's the matter, Chelsea? Why did you act that way?"

"I don't know," she groaned. "There is just something about that man; everything tingles in his presence and I get tied up in knots."

"I'm not surprised," Beth laughed. "He's charming and super handsome."

Chelsea gave her a sour look. "I'm pretty sure I didn't mean in *that* way. I mean he puts me on edge, makes me wary, and he should at least show some respect for a member of the board."

"That's a pity, because I'm quite sure by the way he looked at you and the disappointment in his eyes when you slammed the door in his face that you were making him tingle too, but in the good way."

"I did not slam it in his face, he was miles away," Chelsea muttered in her own defense.

"You have to admit, he is drop-dead gorgeous though."

Beth's face filled with an expression of horror, her hand flying to cover her mouth and her cheeks flaming red. "I'm so sorry, Chelsea," she cried through her fingers.

Chelsea's face softened. "Don't be, Beth. The word 'dead' can still be used in sentences around here, it isn't against company regulations. In fact, sometimes I wish people wouldn't tiptoe around me so much and avoid mentioning Clark. It might be nice to talk about him and reminisce about him with others, not just by myself. It sometimes feels like everyone else is pretending he never existed."

Beth reached out and placed a hand atop Chelsea's, which were clasped together on top of her desk. "I'm sure they only do it to protect you. If you ever want to talk, you could talk with me. I'm always here for you."

"Thanks, Beth, I appreciate that and I might just take you up on it sometime. Now, as for that arrogant man, I don't have to admit whether he's drop-dead gorgeous as you say or not!"

"Okay, maybe not, but I bet you thought it."

"Well, maybe when I first saw him it crossed my mind, but then he opened his mouth and spoiled it all."

"Story of most men!"

The two laughed together and Beth, satisfied that Chelsea was all right, took her leave saying she'd better get back to work. Chelsea agreed that she should do the same; she was ahead of the game and didn't want to lose her advantage.

She picked up the next manuscript on her desk, unfastened the clip and flipped through it, studying the margin notes left by the other team members.

Something seemed odd. The initials at the bottom of the notes didn't belong to anyone on her team. She shrugged—must be a cross-genre novel that someone else had worked on before deciding it belonged in her department. She hoped it wouldn't be too much of a mix; those were hard to place and harder still to market.

She was even more confused after she'd read the first few chapters. When a novel had already been approved, she never read a synopsis or character list first; she liked to get straight into a book with no advance knowledge.

She wanted to see if it grabbed her attention and made her want to continue reading. She liked to get to know who was who as she went, learning about them as the story progressed, just as a reader would do.

This book was set in a futuristic world and the characters were mainly cyborgs if one could categorize them, humans enhanced with technology to survive in a post-apocalyptic world. At first, the characters were young kids and it read very much like a children's book, possibly stretching as far as the young adult genre as the characters aged.

As she read on, however, the themes were decidedly darker, with many intergalactic battles and civil wars among the remaining races of Planet Earth, the injuries and lost characters being far too much for children to handle. She could see why this one had everyone confused.

She had to confess she was completely engrossed. It was a clever and intriguing writing style—the prose around the dialogue matched the age of the characters, growing and maturing with them. The more she read, the more she couldn't tear herself away.

When she came to the build-up to the final battle, she had a sinking feeling. The main protagonists who had been childhood friends and remained so until their late teens—when their relationship developed into romantic love—were about to be separated.

He needed to go to battle, and, as one of the strongest female warriors, she was required to stay back and protect the other women and children. Chelsea dreaded what was coming, but she couldn't stop reading.

An hour later, tears streamed down her face as the battle was won but the main character's life was lost. He died a hero's death, saving the day. But he would never return despite the frantic attempts of the field medics who had tried to keep him alive by replacing all the damaged human parts with cybernetics.

In the end, his injuries had been too extensive, and he had died with his love's name on his lips.

As she finished the last line through blurred vision, she dropped her head onto her desk and sobbed her heart out.

CHAPTER SEVEN

An hour later, Chelsea made her way to Courtney's office, the upsetting manuscript under her arm. She had already had Beth call ahead and ensure Courtney was available to see her, so there could be no ignoring her this time.

She waited impatiently as Courtney's assistant buzzed to announce her arrival. Within seconds, the cute, elfin face appeared around the door with a huge grin and a tiny hand waved her in.

"Hey, Chels! What's up?"

"Did you pass this on to Sci-Fi?" Chelsea demanded as she flung the manuscript down on Courtney's desk. Surprise crossed her sister's delicate features but she said nothing, making her way over to her desk to examine the title.

"Oh, yes, that one came to me from Children's. They didn't think it was appropriate, but they really liked it. They wanted to see if we could handle it.

"There were several of us that loved it but didn't think it came under our banner—a bit too dark for our normal romance readers. I decided to send it to your department, Chelsea, but I put a note on it for the team to handle it and not to pass it to you," Courtney explained, feeling a bit defensive.

"There's nothing written on the front matter to that effect. Did you add an extra page with the message?"

"Um, no, I think I used a Post-It®."

"Courtney! No wonder it got lost. You know how many times these things are handled. That Post-It® probably came off within ten minutes of you putting it on."

"So you read it then?"

"Yes I did. Every word of it."

"Since you read it anyway, you might as well tell me what you thought." Courtney tilted her head, showing her mischievous smile that she often used as a tool.

Chelsea gave in; there was no way she could even pretend to stay mad at Courtney. "It hurt a lot reading it, but I thought the book was amazing. Who knew you could care so much about people who are only half-human at the most? It's a real testament to the writing ability; I was completely hooked."

"I know, right?" Courtney enthused. "It's as if on the outside they're just spare parts, but almost as if their very souls have compensated for the lack of humanity there, transcending to a higher place and being much more compassionate and loving than the real humans left on the planet.

"It was if they had a deeper understanding and respect for the gift of life, so much love it couldn't be held inside them. It was pretty much a story about human frailty, showing us the soul could live for an eternity if only the body could last with it."

The sisters stared at each other. "Religion!" they both declared at once.

"Okay, so we both see where this belongs, but could we really get the readers to understand the parables?" Chelsea asked, biting her bottom lip.

"I don't know the answer to that, but I know a man who will."

Chelsea groaned. "Don't tell me you're suggesting I have to go and speak to Kade."

"Why not? He's a really nice guy, and he's got a great sense of humor. He's totally approachable, and that's not all."

"Don't even go there, Courtney, I'm warning you!"

"Okay, I won't, I promise, but only if you take this book to him right now. This has to be published, and if anyone can get the marketing right, he can."

"Fine," Chelsea muttered, rising from the seat she had taken.

"Oh, one thing. Before you go, drink a glass of water. Your eyes are all red and puffy."

"Gee, thanks, Courtney," she said with a mock sarcastic smile as she headed toward the water cooler to take her sister's advice. After downing two cups of water, she headed for the ladies restroom and checked out her reflection in the mirror.

It's not that I care how I look when I see him; she told herself as she splashed cold water on her face to reduce the swelling and puffiness under her eyes. *I just don't want anyone asking questions about why I was crying.*

Satisfying herself that her primping was for that reason alone, she left the bathroom and made her way over to Marketing.

She approached Kade's office tentatively, but his assistant greeted her warmly. She called the woman by name; she obviously knew everyone in the senior offices. Becky was glad to see Chelsea and responded professionally.

"I don't suppose Mr. Richardson would have a spare moment for an impromptu meeting?" she asked, not sure if she hoped for a positive response more than a negative one.

"I'll check for you," the woman replied, disappearing into the inner office without knocking. It seemed rather familiar to Chelsea, but she decided it was none of her business how Kade ran his office. It didn't take long for the assistant to reappear. "He's just wrapping up a video call; he said to go on in."

Chelsea entered, then stopped in her tracks halfway over to his desk. He was still on the call, saying polite goodbyes with a pleasant smile on his face, promising to talk soon and thanking whoever was on the other end for giving him their time.

Her tummy fluttered as she studied his profile but she attributed it to nerves; after all, this was their first business discussion. She fiddled with the manuscript in her hand while she waited.

She watched his computer mouse disappear under his large, masculine hand as he clicked the disconnect button, then almost took a step back as he leaped to his feet and bounded toward her with enthusiasm.

"Miss Carpenter, hello, nice to see you! Welcome to my office."

The exuberance of the greeting once again made her think of dogs, this time of an eager puppy as he shook her hand firmly with a grin on his face. The contact was accompanied by the stutter in her heart and the constriction of her chest, making it hard for her to breathe. Her palms felt warm and clammy and she quickly pulled her hand from his, embarrassed by their condition.

"I'm sorry, Miss Carpenter, I usually run a completely open-door policy for anybody at any time, but the reception was bad on the call so I closed the door to minimize the noise from …"

She held up a hand. "No need to apologize, and please, call me Chelsea."

"Only if you award me the same courtesy and call me Kade." He smiled at her, the penetrating blue eyes instantly warming and softening as he held her gaze.

"Okay, Kade."

She immediately flushed, his name had come out almost in a whisper, making it sound…intimate. She broke the eye contact, pulling herself back to being all business and focusing on the manuscript in her hands.

"I was wondering if you had five minutes free to discuss this," she said, holding up the document as if she were using it as a shield between them.

"Sure, all the time in the world for you, Chelsea. Come and sit down."

She shivered as he said her name; the way it sounded in his smooth voice gave her goose bumps. Thank goodness he had already turned his back to her and didn't see her reaction.

As she watched him walk back to his desk and take his seat, something dawned on her that she should have noticed long before. A Boston accent was probably one of the most recognizable in the U.S., but Kade most definitely didn't have one.

The Utah dialect originated from early migration, northeastern vocabulary blending with a southern influence as it did in many other states. Like the people from those other states, Utahans had added their own little twist to it to create something completely and wonderfully unique.

Hearing him talk now, she could tell that he was definitely a local boy. She hurried to take the offered seat as she noticed he was looking expectantly at her, probably wondering why she was still standing in the middle of his office gawking at him. She sat down, feeling like a fool.

"So, what's so special about this manuscript?" he asked, indicating the thick document she was clutching to her chest as if it were a life jacket.

She somehow managed to pull herself together and get down to business. "It crosses so many genres it's getting handed around the departments as if it were a hot potato.

However, quite a few of us have read it, and we all believe it's definitely worthy of being published. Courtney and I were discussing it earlier, and we both believe it has some strong religious connotations. The problem is we're not sure if they are obvious enough to market it that way."

"Well, placing it under that heading would definitely set a certain expectation for the readers. It might make the message clearer for them, but if it's too subtle, it might just confuse them and cause them to lose trust in us."

"Exactly, which is why we decided to come to you and see what you think."

"I'll take it home and read it tonight so I can be fully informed before making any decisions. I really appreciate you coming to me with this, Chelsea. I had the feeling that perhaps you didn't think that much of me or my abilities, so I'm really glad you trusted me to be involved."

"I can't deny your qualifications; I guess this will determine how well you can put what you learned at your fancy school into practice."

Chelsea placed her hands firmly on the desk and rose quickly, not wishing to get into the discussion he was trying to initiate. She was mortified to see two damp patches left behind where her hands had been. She marched to the door and was about to open it when an arm reached around her.

As Kade leaned in close to open the door for her, she inhaled a whiff of an intoxicating scent, spicy and masculine. She instantly felt light-headed and staggered a little in her attempt to flee from his office. She headed straight for the bathroom, and leaned over a basin and took deep breaths. She thought over her symptoms, sweaty palms, flushed cheeks, fluttery tummy, racing heart rate, dizziness.

"Oh no, I must be getting sick," she groaned. "Please, Lord, not the flu!"

Great, this all I need. I'd better hide in my office for the rest of the day, and avoid contact with the other employees. When I get home I'll make myself some chicken soup and crawl straight into bed. If I still feel this way come morning, I'll have to consider working from home for a few days. Whatever this is, I don't want to infect everyone in the entire building.

On her way back to her office, she stopped at a vending machine to get a chilled soda, more for placing the can against her burning forehead than to drink. Once back in her office, she didn't feel quite so bad and made it to the end of the day without slowing down on her work.

Leaving that evening, she organized as much work as she could to take home with her, just as a precaution. She was weighed down with paperwork as she exited the main door of the building.

"Please, let me help you with that."

The voice startled her, and she tried to hurry away.

"I'm fine, thanks. My car's just right there."

"They look heavy."

"They are, but I'll manage," she said sharply, trying to keep her distance from Kade. She hadn't turned around to acknowledge him, but with her added load, his long stride was keeping pace with her easily.

She had the sudden urge to drop the files and run, to dive into her car and lock the doors behind her. She knew she was being ridiculous and managed to fight the urge and carry on walking, quickening her pace only slightly.

"Okay, no problem. See you tomorrow," the dejected voice said, fading away as she kept moving.

"Not if I see you first," she muttered to herself, determined to keep her distance from Kade.

She reached her car, dropped the files onto the passenger seat and hurried around to the driver side, falling to the seat and driving off quickly, resisting the urge to look back to see if Kade was still standing in the parking lot watching her departure.

Arriving home, she struggled to get to the front door with her arms piled high with paperwork, reminding her how grateful she was to have picked up that adorable little porch table she'd found at a craft sale in downtown Midway recently. She gladly set the load of manuscripts on the table and unlocked the front door.

She took the files straight through to her bedroom and dropped them on the bed while she went to hunt for the side table she knew she had stored somewhere. It was one of those that resembled a hospital table, designed to slip under the bed and move in front of the occupant.

She had bought it in a daze one night when she had been haunted by dreams of Clark and got up to watch TV at some ridiculous hour. Vulnerable and miserable, she had been seduced by the late night shopping channel, the only thing showing that she could stand to watch at that hour.

She felt vindicated that the table was finally going to be taken out of its box and put to use. She located it in the back of the hall closet, set it up and moved the files onto it along with a few pens and her laptop, then headed to the kitchen to make the chicken soup she had promised herself.

While the soup was heating, she quickly changed into her pajamas, then snuggled into her warm bed with the soup and work sharing space on the new bed table. She would say her prayers later, when she got up to brush her teeth before going to sleep. She was so engrossed in her work she didn't even notice that she felt absolutely fine.

CHAPTER EIGHT

"I can see Kade heading this way," Beth whispered into the intercom.

"Not again!" Chelsea exploded.

"Shall I send him in when he gets here?"

"I guess so," she replied, resigned. "I ran out of excuses a long time ago."

Ever since the day she had approached him about that book, Kade had frequently found excuses to come to see her. She'd begun to wonder if perhaps phones were outlawed in Boston, as many of his questions could have been resolved with a thirty-second call or even an email.

Heck, some of them were so trivial, the janitor would have been able to answer them! Looking at her watch she realized it was 4 on a Friday afternoon. *I thought I had managed to escape this week, but here he comes, about to make his entrance yet again.*

She had forced herself to spend the last few weeks examining her reactions to the man. When she woke up and realized she wasn't sick that morning, she thought at first that the TLC she'd given herself had done the trick, but when her symptoms returned the very moment she saw him again, she'd to admit there was more going on.

It was only fair and right that she sort this out in her head. It was her problem, and she had to face up to it and deal with it.

She considered the way Kade made her feel on edge, wary of him, and the way she wanted to run from him that day in the parking lot. Did she fear him? She didn't think he was a serial killer or a psychopath, but yes, something within her feared him.

Despite her reservations, she needed to discover the reason why. When she allowed herself to closely examine her reactions, she remembered a time when she'd experienced them before. Every time she saw Clark.

The very thought terrified her. She wasn't given to random physical attraction, even if someone did look like a poster-boy male model. After a long, heartfelt talk with God in the privacy of her Sundance sanctuary home, He had helped her admit to herself that she felt drawn to Kade the way she had initially been drawn to her fiancé.

When she met Clark, she'd known instantly they would fall in love. It was hard to explain, but it was as if their souls recognized one other and wanted to be together. There'd been no point fighting it; she didn't *want* to fight it. She went along for the glorious, wonderful ride, falling deeply in love just as she knew she would all along. Was it happening again?

Well, this time she would fight. There was no way she could go through the pain and heartache of loss again. Falling in love with someone else was absolutely out of the question for her. She'd had her time, fleeting as it had been.

Clark was her man—her one and only man. Never again would she open herself up to be hurt. She was done with that. Besides, the reaction she felt in Kade's presence filled her with guilt now that she recognized it for what it was. She was being disloyal to Clark, sullying his memory, cheapening what they'd had together.

She couldn't help how she reacted, but she could do her best to honor Clark by keeping her distance from the other man. The only problem was that he seemed determined to seek her out and make the task she had set for herself almost impossible.

"Kade Richardson to see you, Chelsea," the voice buzzed over the intercom. Chelsea could hear the smile in Beth's voice, knowing she was charmed by him.

Chelsea put on her best game face, steeling her heart, ready for the encounter. "Send him in."

"Hey there." Kade greeted her enthusiastically as he entered the office. He made his way over to her desk, his stunning blue eyes shining with excitement. "I see we've been paired up as trust buddies on the team-building course."

"Team building?" Chelsea screeched. "What team-building course?"

"Oh, I take it you haven't read the memo then."

"Way to go stating the obvious," she muttered. She knew she was being unnecessarily harsh, but it was her only defense in dealing with the situation. "Some of us actually have work to do and don't spend our time watching for emails or gadding about the office chatting." *And charming all the female employees.*

To give him his due, Kade didn't flinch at her words or alter his expression. "I'll give you the general rundown then. Grace has booked one of the best organizational consultants in the business to spend time with us, taking us out in groups of six. We're going for a hike up Mt. Timpanogos to the waterfall—isn't that amazing?"

"Not really, I see it every day," she exaggerated. Though she lived on that mountain and saw Timpanogos every day of her life, she couldn't actually see the falls from her condo.

"Okay, well I haven't really. I've wanted to, but it seemed kind of silly going up there on my own. I know lots of people over in Salt Lake, but I haven't really had time to make any friends here. I think it would feel lonely having that beauty around you and no one to share it with so I've put it off. Anyway, we've been paired up within the groups and you're my partner; isn't that great?"

"Terrific."

If Kade picked up on her sarcasm, he didn't acknowledge it, merely carried on. "So we're going not this Saturday but next, and the memo gives us a list of gear we'll need. Apparently we can buy or rent it all locally, and the company is picking up the tab. I'm really excited about this."

Before Chelsea could respond, which might have been just as well, her door burst open and a handsome face appeared there.

"Surprise!" the man yelled as he stretched his arms in a welcoming expanse.

"Oh, my word! What are you doing here?" Chelsea squealed as she leaped off her seat to greet her visitor. The tall, handsome man strode to meet her halfway, lifting her off her feet and swinging her around before embracing her in a huge bear hug.

Chelsea caught only a fleeting glimpse of the pained and disappointed expression on Kade's face as he retreated from the office, mumbling about giving them privacy.

"I had some great news that I couldn't wait to share," Carter said, finally letting her go. "I've been nominated for the Cartwright Architectural Award! I don't really expect to win, but I'm the youngest to ever be nominated, so it's really a big deal."

"That's amazing, I'm so happy for you!" Chelsea said, going back for another hug.

"Besides, when I last spoke to Mom, she said you hadn't been yourself lately, that you were a little out-of-sorts. I was worried about you, so I decided those two reasons were enough for me to hop a plane and pay a visit this weekend. Surprised?"

"We're honored! Two visits within six months; that's a record for you," Chelsea laughed. "You didn't have to come on my account, I'm absolutely fine, but it's great to see you. And the whole family is going to be stoked about the nomination! I foresee a special celebration dinner tomorrow at Mom's house."

"I hope so. My cooking can't compete with Maggie's."

"Now we're getting down to the real reason you're here," Chelsea teased.

"Well, maybe." Carter grinned. "But I'd like to forego even Maggie's cooking tonight, if you'll let me. Instead of going to Mom's, can I stay over at your place? I'd like to spend some time with just the two of us, like we used to do when we were kids."

Chelsea hesitated for a second. Her apartment had been her private sanctuary for so long, she wasn't sure if she was ready for it to be invaded, even by her beloved twin.

"Hey, don't worry about it; I'll go to Mom's," he said, picking up on her reluctance.

His words made her realize how selfish and unappreciative she was being. He had come all this way from San Francisco mostly because he was worried about her, and she was shutting him out. "Of course you can stay with me; it'll be great fun."

Carter grinned at her change of heart. "We can pretend we're back in the tree house that Dad built for us, hiding from the rest of the world, sharing our secrets. Let's go and get some soda and chips, maybe even some candy. Remember how we used to sneak in and raid the kitchen, eating our monthly allowance of treats in one afternoon?"

Chelsea laughed at the memory. "Yes, and I remember how sick I used to feel afterwards too!"

Carter's face fell in his dramatic way. "I'd forgotten about that part; must have blanked it out. Never mind, we'll limit our supplies this time," he added, brightening at the thought. "I'll go drop in on Mom, tell her I'm here, and let her know my plans for tonight. Shall I tell her to expect you for dinner tomorrow?"

"Yes, I'll be there. Congratulations again on the award—I'm so proud of you."

"Thanks. Come and get me when you're done for the day. I took a cab from the airport, so you're my ride."

"Will do, catch you later."

The rest of the day passed quickly and Chelsea was looking forward to the evening, although she was still a little apprehensive about her fortress being breached.

Picking up Carter, they headed off together, stopping first at Kneaders for the homemade breads they'd quickly come to love when the stores began popping up all over Utah, and then on to Smith's, choosing something for dinner as well as an array of snacks that Chelsea usually forbade herself. It was a celebration, after all.

Carter was like a kid in a candy store checking out her place. He raved about architectural points that went totally over her head, but she was happy to see him happy. Once he had explored every inch of the condo, they went into the kitchen to cook dinner together, the teasing and joking reaching a level where they once again narrowly avoided a food fight.

The meal was fun, and afterwards Chelsea made hot chocolate and suggested they take it out onto the deck.

The night was a little chilly, so she returned to retrieve a sweater for herself and then went to the closet in the spare room for something to keep Carter warm.

She stood in front of the closet, door open, staring at the items inside. She didn't have many of Clark's things—it wasn't as if they had ever lived together or anything.

His folks had let her into his room in their home, telling her to help herself to whatever she wanted. She remembered how numb she had been when she had gathered together some of his favorite books and took a few items of clothing she had loved to see him in, things he'd worn during a particularly wonderful day out, items that carried his scent.

When she reappeared with her small armful of mementos, Clark's parents had protested, telling her she should take more. She didn't want to. She didn't really need them; she could recall every moment, every word, every kiss, without having things to remind her.

Despite her protests, his dad had dashed back into the bedroom and retrieved the photograph of the two of them together that Clark kept on his nightstand. He thrust the frame on top of her pile and she nodded, silently agreeing to take it and thanking him.

Now she picked it up and looked at it. They had been so happy together. The picture caused her too much pain—she couldn't cope with seeing it—and so she had tucked it away in the guest room and tried to forget about it.

She smiled as she ran a finger over their happy laughing faces pressed close together, realizing the pain wasn't nearly so intense now. She was finally beginning to be able to remember the good times with fondness, not the feeling that someone had hacked her heart open with a blunt knife.

She replaced the photo on the table and turned her attention to the three items of Clark's clothing she had chosen. One was a dark grey fleece jacket, ideal for warding off the slight chill that could still come along with the darkness.

There were still a few weeks to go before the nights turned toward balmy, especially up here high in the mountains. She took the jacket from the hanger, pressing it to her face and inhaling deeply, even though she knew that Clark's scent had long since begun fading away.

She'd spent months wearing this around the house, comforted and torn apart by the faint hint of his cologne and his masculine scent that lingered there. She thought of the nights she'd laid in her bed, clutching the fabric to her face, sobbing into it for hours, wailing out her pain, the scents triggering her memory banks to their maximum capacity. Eventually, his essence had faded completely from the jacket, probably diluted by her tears.

She had sorrowfully run the item through the wash before hanging it up and closing the door on it. All she could smell now was the faint remains of the detergent and fabric softener. Closing the closet door, she walked back out to Carter, handing him the fleece.

He looked at it and then looked up into her face. He obviously recognized it. "Are you sure?"

"I'm sure."

"Thanks," he said simply, putting the jacket on and snuggling inside it. He stared at the amazing view from her deck. She sat down at the round wooden table, part of the furniture set she had picked up especially for this area.

"This place is terrific! I love it. What does everyone else make of it?"

"No one's been here to see it; you're the first."

Carter tried to hide his shock, and almost succeeded. She knew that it must be quite a revelation to him, considering how close their family was. The fact that she hadn't invited any of them here, and the fact that none of them had assumed they were welcome to drop in anytime spoke volumes about her emotional state when she'd moved here. "I suppose I should be honored then," he said, all joking aside.

"Well, if anyone was going to break down my barriers, it was always going to be my twin, wasn't it?" They both took a minute to dwell on the significance of the moment before she continued. "Carter, can I ask you something?"

"Sure, go ahead," he said easily, taking a sip of his hot chocolate.

Chelsea grabbed a potato chip, nibbling on it while she considered how to word her question. "Do you think we only have one soul mate in our life? That there's only one person out there for each of us?"

"That's a pretty big question, with a lot to consider. I think my simple answer would have to be no."

"What makes you say that?"

"Because I think we have an infinite capacity for love that knows no bounds, and I don't believe that most people are cut out to be alone in this life. Obviously, there are exceptions. Some people choose solitary lives, but I think that's part of the plan.

"For most of us, I think it's natural to have a partner, and we will always hope for that, no matter the circumstances. If you're asking if you can love someone else yet still love Clark, then I believe the answer is yes."

Chelsea gasped. "I never mentioned me or Clark! It was a just a general question."

"Chelsea, I'm your twin, remember? We don't need words between us to explain things. I'm right, aren't I?"

Chelsea rubbed the bridge of her nose, wondering if she was really ready to discuss this. Putting it into words would make it all the more real, really force her to admit to herself that she was recovering, finally dealing with the loss of Clark, and taking the first tiny steps toward moving on.

It was a frightening thought. Clark was the only man she had ever dated, the only man she had ever considered dating. It didn't matter at the moment that Kade might be in a relationship or have no interest in dating her, the issue was whether she could even consider another relationship.

She had spent so long putting up her armor and keeping her shields in place, how would it feel to let them all go? Deciding there was no one better to talk it through with than someone who would understand everything she was saying, no matter how little she said, she let herself confide in Carter.

"There's this new guy at work, and from the moment I met him, I just had a feeling I shouldn't trust him and was afraid of him, but everything about him always checked out. Everyone else thought he was great, and he hadn't given me any reason to feel the way I did.

"I just always seemed to be over-emotional around him, angry, annoyed, and scared; you know, hypersensitive to every little thing he said or did."

Carter nodded, encouraging her to go on.

"I kept him at arm's length, was downright mean to him sometimes, and it was for that reason that I really had to examine what I was feeling, because it wasn't fair and just wasn't Christian."

She looked helplessly at Carter, hoping he would understand what she was getting at.

"I can't really imagine you being mean to anyone, but I know exactly where you are coming from. You did the right thing in the end, even though it took you a while to get there. So what did you find when you allowed yourself to be honest about your feelings?"

"Well, once I got over thinking that I was getting sick every time I saw him," she rolled her eyes thinking how stupid she'd been, "I realized I was afraid of him, but not because of anything he had done or might do. I was afraid of him because of the way I felt about him.

"It was me I was scared of, not him. I was petrified that my carefully-built walls and defenses would be shattered into a million pieces. I'm still worried that if they break, I'll break again too. I was such a mess, Carter! If I let all the feelings in again, I might go back to that."

"Chelsea, you're much stronger than you think you are. I truly believe that you've been letting those barriers down slowly all the time.

"Look at us right now. I'm here; you've let me into your sanctuary and into your head and heart. I'm sitting here wearing Clark's fleece, and you're actually okay with that. Don't you think that all your senses are telling you that you might be ready to move on now, and that's why you're so afraid?"

"You could be right, but what if I get hurt again? What if I'm rejected, or what if I fall in love and something terrible happens a second time?"

Carter shuffled his chair a little closer to Chelsea's and put an arm around her shoulder. "I honestly don't think that's going to happen, but if it does, you'll come through it the same way you came through it last time.

"With our love and God's love, and with the help of our extended family at church, you'll pull through, just as the Carpenters always do. Everything happens for a reason, you know that. Every life lesson we learn brings us a little closer to Him."

They both sat quietly thinking, each taking a big sip of hot chocolate.

"Can I suggest you think of it in a different way? What if this guy is His plan for you, the path you're meant to be on? Would you really want to turn away from that, reject it and decide you can't take the risk and prefer to walk your own path, alone?"

"No!

Rejecting the path I'm meant to follow would be like pushing Him out of my life!"

"So the answer is simple. Ask Him, pray for the Spirit to guide you, let go of the fear, and look at the signs. You know He'll show you if this is the direction you're meant to follow. You can't live in fear of emotions; that's like rejecting all the gifts that are given to us. Living in an emotional desert of your own making is no life at all."

"So you don't think I'm being disloyal to Clark?"

"No, absolutely not. Clark has moved on, and so should you. All he would want for you is happiness, and because he isn't here to make you happy, then he would wish for someone else to do it for him."

Chelsea felt a great weight lifted from her heart, the burdens she had been carrying inside letting go. She began to cry, and once she started, she couldn't stop.

"Let it all out, Chelsea. I'm here for you, just let it all go," Carter whispered soothingly as he held her close.

CHAPTER NINE

Chelsea woke the next morning feeling much lighter of heart. She wouldn't say she was healed; she was far from ready to thrust Clark from her memories as if he had never existed, but she was ready to consider the possibility of a future for herself.

Maybe there was a glimmer of hope after all. Maybe she didn't have to keep her heart sealed off from emotion. Maybe, just maybe, she really did have more than work, church and family that could fill her life and banish her loneliness.

She did what she knew she should have done from the moment she had flared with unreasonable anger and suspicion against the stranger in the interview chair. She'd opened even the most secret parts of her heart in prayer, and begged for forgiveness for having closed them off, even to God.

She hadn't been able to face being guided to a new path when the one she was on previously had been ripped from under her feet. She didn't want to know, hadn't allowed herself to be given direction.

It was a big failing on her part, but she knew He would understand that it had been the only way to make it through the loss. For all she knew, it was what He required of her—to find her own way through and deal with it with only His comfort to soothe her.

She had never faltered from that, never failed to see that He was with her always, but she had been blanking out His signs that she was ready to move on now.

She wasn't going to actively pursue a relationship with Kade or anyone else, but she opened every last fragment of her heart and soul to her leading light, ready to be taken in whichever direction He saw fit and knowing that

He would never steer her wrong. She wasn't going to fight any more. She came out of denial and was ready to face up to her feelings, living with their consequences, whatever they may be.

If she suffered more heartbreak, then so be it. She would come out the other end closer to Him than ever.

Feeling more peaceful inside than she had in two years, she headed for the shower.

Once dressed, she found an impatient Carter out on the deck. "Come on! If we get to Mom's quickly, we might just be in time for Maggie's amazing breakfast."

"You and your stomach!" Chelsea laughed. "I still feel full from the junk we ate last night."

"Come off it, you nibbled on a few potato chips like a squirrel with a nut!"

"If you say so. Let's get the Golden Boy home to receive his accolades and adoration," she teased, giving him a playful nudge.

Carter was quiet on the journey—unusually so.

"Anything wrong?" she asked, keeping her eyes on the road.

"No, nothing at all," he was quick to reply. "You seem much happier today."

"I am. Thank you for last night, I really needed to hear everything you said."

"That's what brothers are for, right?"

"That, and putting worms in their sister's beds."

"Hey, I only did that once, and we were, like, five or something at the time."

"Once was enough! It was such a big fat worm that I thought it was a snake. I couldn't use my Cinderella bed sheets you ruined with that worm ever again. It made me shiver with fear every time I saw them after that, and they were my favorites, too."

"I'll tell you what, if I can find them in queen size, I'll buy you a new set. How's that?"

"I think you might struggle, but I'll take the offer. If you can find them, I want them."

They grinned at each other; everything was right in their world.

The day with the family in attendance at the house had been great fun as always, and now they sat around the dining table, reaching the end of an excellent meal provided by Maggie. Even Cassie had ventured down from her ivory tower, tearing herself away from her laptop to join them.

"So what's up with this team building malarkey, Mom?" Chelsea asked after waiting for the attention on Carter to finally settle down so she could quiz Grace for details.

"You're breaking the rules, Chelsea. No work talk at the dinner table."

"I wouldn't call this work talk specifically. Besides, you're making me do it on a Saturday so it falls strictly into the extracurricular category."

"I suppose you have a point. I'll let you off this time," Grace smiled. "Did you read the memo?"

"Not yet. I just heard about it when this great oaf beside me barged into my office without so much as a courtesy knock and distracted me."

Carter chuckled quietly, happy to see his sister fully immersing herself into the good-natured banter and insults that were the family's way of displaying how much they loved each other.

"Okay, I'll tell you a little about it then. Stephen Blake is the leading expert in his field right now. He's renowned for really bringing people together, for getting them to really invest and trust in their team members and remove the element of competition and one-upmanship that often exists within an office environment."

"I don't think we have any of those types of problems at Carpenter Global. Everything runs like clockwork, the teams work great together, and the different departments respect each other's abilities. They know how to utilize the talents available and not waste time trying to prove that one is better than the other. We're all working toward the same shared goal."

"I totally agree. It only takes one person to react badly to something to bring about discontent, compromising the smoothly-running operations. I've also heard how those things can snowball, and we're lucky we don't have much of it within our firm."

"So why this, and why now?"

"It was an idea that popped into my head, and you know I always follow gut instincts. It just seemed like a good time, in case there was any underlying and unspoken resentment toward Kade and the new position, although I would hope that everyone would feel comfortable enough to speak out if they weren't happy."

"I can see where you're coming from, but as far as I know, Kade has made himself everybody's friend and everyone loves him. Have you heard differently?"

"Now you can't deny that this is specific work talk. Let's just say that it can't do any harm to cement the bonds that exist and give some people a fun day out reconnecting with nature. He's taking the groups up the mountain to the waterfall, incorporating the team-building exercises along the way. Many of them will be getting a day out of the office; you just got unlucky that it falls on a Saturday."

"Thanks a lot, Mom. You might have swung it so I got a working day out of the office too! Honestly, is there any point in working for the family business if you can't get any perks?"

Everybody laughed at Chelsea's mock whine, and the conversation moved on. As Cassie left to return to her writing and Carter and Courtney disappeared into the family room, Chelsea and Grace were left alone.

"Mom, would you take a walk with me out to the stables?"

"Sure, let's just help clear the table and start the dishes or Maggie will do it all before we get back, even if we do tell her to leave it until we return. Then she can get on with her evening as well."

They quickly cleared the dishes and left when Maggie insisted she could finish wiping the counters and closing down the kitchen.

Chelsea met Grace at the back door and they headed off at a slow saunter, appreciating the still and pleasant night. The horses began to whicker gently as they heard the women approach, and Chelsea ducked into the barn to gather a pocketful of treats.

Taking time to fuss and feed each velvet muzzle that peered over the stall door, she pondered how she was going to start the conversation. As usual, Grace gave her the opening she needed.

"You weren't just afraid to come down here alone in the dark. I'm assuming you wanted to talk to me in private?"

Chelsea chuckled. "Spot on as ever." Her smile faded and she took a deep breath. "Mom, do you think anyone would consider it wrong for me to, um, well…move on?"

Grace hesitated before answering. "Just to make sure we're on the same page, we are talking about Clark?"

Chelsea nodded, afraid to speak, hoping her mom would see the gesture in the half light.

"In that case, I would first have to say that what others think is of no consequence; it's what you think that matters. It's been two years; you have grieved for him more than we could all bear to see. You've shut yourself down and cut yourself off, even from us, and I would have to say I'd be overjoyed to have my daughter back, whole and complete. Let me ask you— do you feel it's the right time, and do you feel it's right with God?"

"I think He's been trying to tell me that it's time for a while now, but I'm ashamed to say I denied it. Only very recently, and thanks to Carter, I'm beginning to feel as if I might be ready."

"I was surprised when Carter said he was being allowed to penetrate your fortress," Grace said wryly. "Seriously though, I'm incredibly glad he was such a help to you and am very pleased to hear that you're finally healing. Everyone who loves you only wants to see you happy. We'll all support you. I can't imagine why anyone wouldn't. In the end, we both know that there is only one fit to judge, so what does it matter?"

"Thanks, Mom. Like Carter last night, you just said everything I needed to hear."

"Happy to help. Now, since it's just you, me, and the horses, is there someone specific that initiated this chain of events?"

"Yes and no. There is someone I might have developed some feelings for, but I managed to ignore them. Really, it was only last night when things started to make more sense to me. Up until that point, I didn't even know what was going on with me, never mind trying to assess what was going on with him."

"I can see that this way of feeling is still very new to you, and a little frightening, so I won't pry if you're not ready."

"No, it's okay. It's Kade."

"Our Kade? Ahh," Grace drew it out, shaking her head. "Now things are beginning to make sense. I can't believe I didn't see it for myself."

"What makes sense?"

"It hadn't escaped my notice that there was a certain friction between you two; it was partly what prompted me to think about hiring Stephen Blake. Now I understand that it was less conflict and more captivation."

"I wouldn't go that far!"

"Well, you have to admit he's very…eligible." The tone of her voice and the look she gave Chelsea suggested that 'eligible' wasn't the word she really wanted to use!

"Mom!" Chelsea laughed, admonishing her mother. "Don't have me married off just yet. I don't even know if he likes me, never mind if I'm actually ready to date. I haven't exactly been sweetness and light around him either."

In the growing dark, Chelsea completely missed Grace's knowing smile. "Come on, let's give the rest of the horses their treats before they kick their stall doors down."

After ensuring each horse had his share of petting and treats, the two women linked arms and made their way back up to the house, content to walk together in silence.

As they reached the back door, Chelsea had a sudden urge she couldn't help but give in to.

"You go on in; I'll be back in a few minutes."

"I'll be in the family room with the others," Grace called as she went inside.

Chelsea made her way around to the pool area, crossing over the sun deck and heading for the guesthouse. As she suspected, the uppermost light was on, letting her know that Cassie was awake and working.

She knocked lightly on the door. There was no answer so she knocked a little harder. It only took a minute for the usually disheveled Cassie to yank the door open, a scowl on her face. Her features softened when she saw it was her sister standing there.

"That's a relief. I thought it was Carter here to raid my snacks and wind me up."

"It wouldn't have surprised me either, so don't rule it out, but it's only me at the moment."

Cassie stepped back and held the door open wide. "Come on in."

Chelsea shook her head. "I can see you're working and I don't want to disturb you. I just wanted to ask you something."

"Okay, what is it?"

"You know you said you were going to save a copy of each book for me?"

Puzzlement caused Cassie's brow to wrinkle. "Yes, why?"

"If you've got the first one here, can I have it now?"

Chelsea watched as the confusion turned to shock, then sheer joy lit up her sister's beautiful features. She nodded at her frantically before turning and bounding up the stairs, taking them two at a time. Chelsea heard footsteps pounding across an upstairs room.

Then before she knew it, Cassie appeared on the stairs again, barreling down at top speed. She proudly thrust the hardback book toward Chelsea, who took it and hugged it close to her.

"Thank you, this really means a lot."

"You're more than welcome. I'm almost too excited for words thinking you're going to finally read it."

"Nothing leaves you lost for words for long," Chelsea teased. "I'll let you get back to work, but thanks again. I'll tell you what I think when I finish it." She gave Cassie a big hug, turned, and began to walk away.

"Hey, how did you know I was working?" Cassie called after her.

Chelsea whirled back to face her sister. "Look in the mirror," she called, with a wicked grin on her face. Smiling to herself, she crossed back over the pool area. She had often wondered how Cassie managed to get any writing done as she seemed to spend an extraordinary amount of time running her hands through her hair.

The luxuriously thick, blonde mane she had inherited from Grace always ended up pumped up to the max and sticking out at wild angles all over the place. Whenever she wrote, Cassie ended up looking like a scarecrow.

Deciding to stay over that night made sense. It was getting late and she would be meeting the family for church early tomorrow anyway since Carter was in town. Going home just didn't make sense.

The thoughts surprised her. Normally after spending so much time pretending to be upbeat and happy, she was more than ready to run back to the solitude of her own place.

That's definitely a step in the right direction, she thought as she prepared for bed. After saying her prayers, she snuggled under the covers and picked up her sister's first romance novel.

The cover depicted a beautiful woman being held captive at sword point by a very handsome, swashbuckling man. The main clue to his being a pirate was the skull and crossbones flag flying from the mast of the wooden ship they stood aboard—not an eye patch or wooden leg in sight. *Okay*, Chelsea thought, taking deep, calming breaths as she opened the book to the first page.

Now for the real test.

CHAPTER TEN

Chelsea went through the checklist one more time before stowing everything she needed for the hike in her backpack. She had been born and raised in this area, and like many who lived in this amazing setting, she was quite outdoorsy.

She had no need to rent or buy any of the gear mentioned in the memo; she was already equipped to climb mountains higher than Mt. Timpanogos, which she had climbed before to see the falls up close.

She'd had a pleasant week at work, despite her disappointment that Kade had kept his distance. It was typical that now that she was ready to stop blaming him for her feelings, his impromptu visits to her office had suddenly stopped for no good reason.

Never mind, she would see him today. She wasn't sure if she was going to bring up her unfair treatment and apologize for it or just demonstrate by her actions that she had changed. She would wait to see how the day progressed and how much she and Kade were together as "trust buddies," to use Stephen's buzz words.

As horrified as she was when she first heard about this, now she was really looking forward to it. She was excited about the climb to the waterfall and excited about seeing Kade. She was sure she could live without the Stephen Blake exercises, but she would throw herself into them wholeheartedly anyway.

She was all set to go, but it was too early to leave. She paced around her condo, unsure of what to do with herself. She was already wearing her well-broken-in hiking boots, and her footsteps were heavy as she walked around, trying to calm her enthusiasm.

She went into the kitchen, poured herself a glass of juice, and took it out to the deck. She chuckled as she looked over toward the location of Stewart Falls. It seemed so silly to be driving down to the foot of the mountain to hike back up when she could actually cross the terrain and reach it from here a lot quicker.

Still, she had an unfair advantage, and using it would defeat the whole purpose of the day. She would have to remind herself of that when it came time to follow the trail back down only to collect her car and drive back up.

The course wasn't over until they reached the bottom, so she would need to stick with the group; not that she thought she would want to leave early, not now.

It seemed to take forever, but eventually she was standing at the foothills with Martha, Stuart, and Paul, who were already there when she arrived. She chatted with them but kept an eye on the arriving cars, eager to catch a glimpse of Kade when he showed up.

When she did spot him, her heart stopped, fluttered, then raced in her chest while butterflies danced in her tummy. This time she knew she wasn't getting sick; how ridiculous that thought had been! She reveled in the feelings he stirred within her and waited to greet him with a warm and open smile as he approached the group.

"Hi, everyone, are we all looking forward to this?"

Chelsea felt let down as everyone responded enthusiastically. He had only glanced quickly in her direction before averting his gaze and hadn't addressed her directly or approached her.

Perhaps she was mistaken, but he had always been so eager to see her before, deliberately seeking her out. She held hopes that he liked her, maybe was even attracted to her. He showed no signs of that today. In fact, he seemed almost distant as he chatted and laughed with the others, never looking her way.

Jessica was the last to arrive, quickly followed by Stephen Blake, the man himself. Before they moved, he gave them a long (and boring, if she was being honest) motivational speech and pep talk, then explained his goals for the team today. Chelsea barely took any of it in. She had built this day up so much, and now it looked like it was going to be a total disaster.

She knew she had no one to blame but herself. He was obviously sick of being treated badly by her and was no longer willing to go the extra mile to make peace. It hurt, but it was understandable, so she would just have to suck it up and deal with it.

As they began to move, Chelsea tried to cheer herself with the sights and sounds of nature, but the man just kept droning on in his monotone voice. From the parts she picked up, a lot of what he was saying did ring true, but it all seemed like common sense to

Chelsea, only with a few key phrases, buzzwords, and some pretentious psychobabble thrown in to make it sound more impressive and unique.

He must have had excellent references before Grace Carpenter had let him loose on her staff. Chelsea occupied her thoughts wondering how he had managed it, considering he seemed to have nothing new to offer (in her humble opinion).

Stephen Blake came to a halt as they reached a small stream, probably created by a run-off. It wasn't deep and was only about twelve inches wide. The bank on this side was low, almost level with the stream, but the bank on the other side was perhaps eighteen inches higher.

"This is perfect," Stephen declared. "Let's begin the first exercise in confidence and problem solving. Is there anyone here who thinks they can stand at the bank and step up onto the other bank without getting their feet or any other part of their body wet?"

Her interest piqued, Chelsea considered the challenge. She could step over the water easily, and she could probably step up onto the foot-and-a-half bank without leverage, having the required leg muscle strength to push herself up. Combining the two might be a different story.

Starting a foot away from the high step would make a world of difference. In the end, she decided she probably couldn't do it without leaning forward to place her hands on the bank, or pressing down on the leg making the first step. She looked around; Kade and Stuart were the only two that had stepped forward. Paul was hesitating, and the others girls were shaking their heads.

"Are we allowed to take a run at it?" Paul asked, stepping forward to join the other two.

"No, it has to be from a standing position."

"Then I'm out," Paul replied and took a step back.

"Okay, what I have observed here is the split in the group. Two were certain of their limitations, knowing for sure they couldn't do it and letting others take the lead. Two were unsure, giving it prolonged consideration before making their decisions. One accepted the rules of the game and decided after a time that she didn't have the necessary means to complete the task on time. The other questioned the rules, but when they were enforced, he accepted them and stepped back. Two were instantly confident in their capabilities and took the lead.

"Now, let's all forget about what your jobs actually are and where your skills and qualifications are already put to use. Imagine you are given a rough first draft that you have to have in the stores by Christmas.

"How would you organize yourselves as a team to maximize your efficiency and complete the task, taking into account only the personality traits you have just displayed?"

Chelsea grinned; this was more like it. This was fun and useful. Maybe this man did have something worthwhile to teach after all. The group broke into a healthy discussion and had soon organized themselves and distributed tasks. Stephen beamed with pride as they explained their thinking and their results.

"Excellent, all of you. Now only one thing remains, and that's for the two who showed absolute faith in their own ability to put their money where their mouths are. Up you go, guys."

The group laughed and Kade stepped forward, positioning himself on the bank. He reached out with one long leg, placing his foot firmly on the top of the bank at the other side of the stream, making sure he had his balance.

Chelsea couldn't help but notice how the fabric of his washed out, faded denim jeans stretched over his muscular thighs and rear end as he held the position. She flushed at her own thoughts, shocked by her own audacity but still unable to tear her eyes away from the delightful view.

Once Kade was sure he had the position of his foot just right and his balance in check, he launched himself off the low bank. He wobbled for just a second, but he flung an arm out to stabilize himself and ended up on top of the higher bank.

He turned to face the group, and Chelsea filled with pride and joined in the applause as he took a theatrical bow, playing it up for their amusement.

Stuart was the next to go. His confidence was boosted by seeing Kade make it and Chelsea immediately saw the error he made. He hadn't taken the time to ensure his foot was firmly placed on the other side, going for speed and momentum, launching himself quickly with no hesitation.

His right foot had been slightly on the slope of the bank instead of flat on top, and as he launched, he merely served to push himself backwards, his rear end making a small splash as he landed in the tiny stream. He, too, stood up and took a bow to the applause and laughter from the group.

"Well, I guess that taught me a valuable lesson," he grinned sheepishly. "Can I try again?"

"Be my guest," Stephen said, motioning for him to go ahead.

This time, Stuart followed Kade's lead, taking his time and being more cautious, and his second attempt was successful.

"Congratulations! Now how do you propose getting your teammates across?"

The two men surveyed the remainder of the group. Chelsea burned under Kade's look as he followed her legs from her feet to her waist, assessing their length. "I think for all of them except Martha, it should be easy.

They all have long enough legs to place one foot firmly against the side of the bank, then we take their hands and pull as they launch. We step back as they reach the top, allowing them to get the launch foot on top, and then the other can follow."

"Do you agree with that, Stuart?"

"Absolutely," he nodded.

"Are you sure this time?"

The group chuckled. "Yes, I'm sure," he said, slightly embarrassed but still having fun.

"Okay, so you, Jessica, do you trust Stuart to pull you up?" Stephen asked.

Jessica hesitated. "Not completely; I'm afraid he'll slip and we'll both go down. He slipped before."

"So what do you want to do?"

Chelsea silently willed her to do the right thing while the girl considered her answer.

"I'm going to forget the first failed attempt and trust that he learned all he needed to learn from it. He's going to pull me up and we're going to be fine," Jessica proposed.

"Yes!" Chelsea declared, applauding Jessica along with the rest of them. Stuart beamed, delighted at the show of faith. He pulled her up onto the bank with ease, lifting her into his arms and waltzing off with her on the other side. As their laughing faces reappeared, Stephen asked if Stuart was ready for the next one.

"No, I made myself dizzy doing that! Quite frankly, I wouldn't trust myself close to the edge of the bank, never mind have someone else's safety—and dry clothes—in my hands."

"Good call. Chelsea, go with Kade."

Chelsea gulped and stepped forward. She raised one leg and placed her foot firmly against the bank at the other side. It was almost on the top but not quite, not enough for her to have made it on her own, as she had suspected.

She held out her arms and Kade reached for her. She felt a zing shooting through her body as they touched, and she wobbled on her one foot. He waited until she had steadied herself then he looked her in the eyes for the first time that day.

The piercing gaze made her feel both dizzy and exhilarated. She closed her eyes, then launched. For a split second, it felt like she was hovering in midair, then she felt a firm pull and suddenly she was pressed hard against Kade's masculine chest, inhaling that spicy scent that was all him.

Her legs trembled and her knees weakened, but before she could fall off the low bank into the stream, Kade let go of her hands and wrapped his arms around her, leading her in a step back from the edge and supporting her. She looked up and he stared down at her, their eyes meeting, his smoldering, hers wide and doe-like.

The cheers of their coworkers broke their spell and Kade released her.

"I'm sorry," he muttered, averting his gaze again. "I forgot to step back as you came up. There was hardly enough room for the two of us so I had to grab you before you fell."

"That's all right, thank you for rescuing me."

Kade looked down at the eighteen-inch drop. "It was hardly life or death, only wet feet," he muttered.

"Or a wet backside," she added playfully.

She thought she saw a flicker in his eyes and a hint of a smile twitch at one corner of his mouth, but he turned away quickly. Paul had already crossed with Stuart's help, and that left only Stephen and Martha on the other side.

"Okay, this is going great everyone, but what about Martha? Why can't she cross the same way as the others?"

"She's much shorter than the rest of us—she probably couldn't make the stretch," Stuart jumped in quickly.

"She's wearing sneakers, so her foot would slip the moment we pulled," Kade added.

"So what are you going to do, leave her behind?"

"No way," they all protested, almost in unison.

They had all fully invested in the game, seeing the small drop-off and tiny stream as a cavernous ravine into a raging river, a fall certain to lead to serious injury or death, but they weren't going to let their imaginations interfere with practical solutions.

No one was willing to leave a teammate behind, and the group brainstormed frantically to come up with a way to get the tiny Martha across.

"What if I straddle the drop-off and the river, and then lift her across by holding her at the waist?" Kade suggested. "Then I can kind of pass her up to you guys."

They considered the option and nodded, all thinking that the suggestion could work. Questioningly, with eyebrows raised, all eyes turned to Martha, silently asking if she would go along with the idea.

She looked a little scared but nodded bravely. Once Kade was in position, she stepped forward. He double-checked his balance then lifted her with ease, swinging her around where the others quickly grabbed her and pulled her up to safety.

"Now how do I get back up?" Kade laughed. "Am I allowed to go back over to the original side and start again?"

"You tell me," Stephen said sagely. "Is that the most efficient and effective way to finish the task?"

"If something isn't working," Chelsea mused, "it's often quicker and less complicated to scrap it and start over, rather than trying to adapt it to make it work."

"Then again, he's halfway over. Is it worth wasting that effort if there is a solution to reach the goal from there?"

"Possibly so, providing we can find one," Chelsea had to agree.

"I think we can make it work if we attack it hard and fast." Stuart made his way to the edge, standing as close as he dared. "Right Kade, give me your hand."

Kade obliged, stretching his arm out for Stuart to grasp. "What next?"

"On the count of three, you're going to swing with your right leg, hard and fast as you can. As you come round, reach out for the others. They grab and we all pull."

Kade shrugged and grinned, willing to give it a try. The others on the bank looked at each other doubtfully, unsure if it was going to work. Should they put their trust in one person's idea to bring the task to a swift conclusion?

They were all thinking of this as an actual work project, still applying the pretense that they had the novel to produce for the Christmas market. They decided to go for it.

It worked, but Kade's momentum as they yanked knocked most of them over, leaving several of them in a tangled heap of arms and legs up on the bank. They laughed uproariously, trying to unravel themselves from the others and scramble to their feet.

Chelsea blushed furiously, heat flooding through her body as Kade's weight lay atop her, making her wonder what it would be like to experience that without the audience and without the barrier of the clothing they wore.

She kicked furiously and scrambled away on all fours, escaping the situation and forbidden thoughts, still shocked at the effect this man had on her. As she got to her feet, she saw that no one had noticed her sudden discomfort, so she relaxed and joined them in the rowdy celebration of completion of the first task.

The day continued to be great fun, with Stephen leading them in doing frequent exercises in their pre-assigned pairs as they made their way up the mountain. Chelsea had felt shy working one-on-one with Kade, but she soon got over it as they applied themselves completely to the tasks.

The final one before the picnic lunch was a bonding exercise where they had to sit down with each person and just talk about any topic of their choosing for ten minutes before moving on to the next person.

Chelsea had enjoyed learning more about her colleagues from other departments, but she was apprehensive now that it was her turn to approach Kade. She still hadn't decided if she should bring up and apologize for her earlier behavior, but if she intended to, now would be her chance.

"Hey there," he said casually as she sat down beside him.

"Hey!" She kept her head down, picking at the ground and apparently fascinated by what she found there.

"I have a confession to make."

"I think I owe you an apology."

They both spoke at the same time, causing the other to laugh and breaking the tension between them.

"Ladies first," Kade offered.

"Okay, I'll be quick," Chelsea promised. "I owe you an apology. I really haven't been very nice to you since you joined the firm. Not only was it unprofessional, it was downright rude of me, and I'm sorry.

"I want you to know it was nothing personal; it was just an outgrowth of some of my own issues that I was still dealing with. I can't explain them right now, but it was unfair and selfish of me. I can't say how badly I feel about it all, and I hope we can move forward with a much better working relationship in the future."

He smiled at her easily. "Apology accepted, and I'll respect your wishes to not explain any further. I'll be more than happy to move on from it. Besides, you weren't that bad."

"I was!"

"Okay, you were, but it's in the past now, right?"

"Hey, you were supposed to keep denying it!" Chelsea laughed, giving him a playful nudge, then blushed as she realized what she had done.

Why did she feel so comfortable around him now that she wasn't constantly trying to battle with her attraction to him? It was as if she had known him for years, like family, but…more.

"So what was it you were going to say?" she asked quickly, trying to gloss over the moment.

"I was going to say that I had a confession, and also an apology." Kade's face had lost its sparkle and turned serious, almost sad. "From the moment I walked into that interview, I knew you were someone I wanted to get to know. Then I could see that I had upset both you and the CEO talking about Mr. Carpenter.

"It really wasn't my intention to do that; all I wanted to express was how much I admired the man and how much it would mean to work in the firm he created. I wanted to make amends, and I think I tried too hard and pushed too fast, and I'm sorry for that. But the more I saw of you and the more I got to know you, and know about you, the more I longed to ask you out on a date."

Chelsea's heart soared. He liked her! He wanted to ask her out! No, he *longed* to ask her out! She felt like getting up and doing a victory dance with lots of high kicking and cartwheels, cheerleader style.

This day had gone from useful and fun to magical, and if it weren't for the hard ground, she would feel like she was floating on a cloud of happiness.

His next words brought her back down to earth with a crash.

"Of course, I know now that can never happen, but it's great that we can have a fantastic working relationship." He grinned at her and she smiled a thin, watery smile back in his direction.

Why? She screamed at him in her head. *Why did you change your mind? Was I that awful?*

"Great," she agreed weakly, wanting to curl up under a rock and cry. It was typical—she had found a handsome, attractive man who liked her too, and before she could even admit to herself that she might have the capability to love again, she had driven him off by being a total harridan.

"Once we establish a great working connection, maybe we could even go as far as being friends? I still don't really know anyone around here outside of work."

"Yeah, friends, that would be nice." She knew she was sounding like a parrot, mindlessly repeating his words and agreeing, but she couldn't find it within herself to add anything else or to inject any enthusiasm into the conversation at all.

"So now that we've got all that sorted, did you have a nice weekend?"

"Terrific, actually. I had an overnight guest on Friday and a wonderful dinner with my family on Saturday. Then Sunday, of course, I got to spend with my extended family at church. "

She was surprised at the shock that crossed his face at her answer, but he covered it quickly and distracted her with another comment.

"That sounds great. Ditto on Sunday, the rest of the time I just spent working. Like I said, no close friends here yet."

"Do you miss Boston at all?"

"Not really. I miss some of the people I knew there, but not much else. What I was missing the most was all this." He held out a hand, gesturing toward the breathtaking scenery around them.

"You like outdoor pursuits?"

He nodded enthusiastically. "I love riding; I really missed having horses when I was in Boston. I'd like to take that up again when I have the chance. I also love the mountains, hiking, rock climbing—you name it, I do it. I would love to live in a cabin up here, tucked away in the mountainside. Can you imagine waking up to this view and the sound of the falls every morning?"

"I can," Chelsea said.

This conversation was making her feel even worse. It was quickly becoming apparent that on paper, they were a perfect match. They had so much in common, they were close in age, they shared a religion, a love of horses and riding, their work, the outdoors, and he even wanted to live in a place that sounded suspiciously like her condo, darn it.

She'd had an amazing opportunity to connect with someone, and she had blown it through stubbornness and blindness. She had certainly learned some lessons here!

"Time's up," Stephen called. Chelsea rose to move on to the next person, mentally kicking herself for the losses she had brought upon herself.

After the bonding exercise came the final hike up to the bottom of the main falls, where they would stop a distance away and have the picnic lunch they had brought along in backpacks.

The group chatted amicably, and Stephen praised them all for the success of the day. He'd decided to end the session there, feeling this particular group needed no more instruction.

After lunch, they were free to do as they chose. Most decided to head back down in the group, but Kade had other plans.

"I'd like to stick around for a while, enjoy the view, explore a little. Anyone fancy joining me?"

There were no takers, and Chelsea felt sorry for him as his face fell. "I'll stay," she volunteered. "I haven't been up here for a while, and I marked the whole day off in my planner anyway."

She knew she was torturing herself by being in his company more than was strictly necessary, but it seemed the right thing to do. He'd told her on numerous occasions he had no friends here yet, and she knew that the beauty of this place was better shared; she knew that probably better than anyone.

"Great," he responded enthusiastically. "I brought my camera and would love to get some close-up pictures of the falls."

As they said goodbye to the rest of the group, waving cheerily to them as they left to hike back down the trail, Chelsea felt a little awkward standing alone with Kade. "Come on then," she said. "I thought you wanted to get closer to the main attraction."

Kade hurried to follow her, his long legs catching up with her easily. They moved together in silence, the tension gone now that they had a task and a goal to focus on, an easy companionship developing between them in the shared pursuit.

Talk became almost impossible anyway as they reached the edge of the rushing water, which roared in their ears and vibrated through their bodies. They stared at the amazing sight, then grinned at each other in delight.

She smiled as Kade grabbed his camera from his backpack and enthusiastically snapped pictures. She laughingly obliged when he motioned for her to stand next to the falls, including her in the pictures.

She held out her hand for the camera and they swapped places. Hiding behind the camera, she felt safe in admiring the form she saw in the viewfinder.

Tall and lean, dressed in hiking boots and jeans and a sweater, he was the epitome of masculinity. She didn't know which one was the greatest example of God's amazing creations, Kade or the falls.

She took more pictures than necessary, not wishing to give up her perfect excuse to stare at him and drink him in. She didn't fight the butterflies or the shortness of breath that always occurred when she looked at him; she went along with it, reveling in her new and recent awakening that she never thought would happen again.

Rather than bringing pain, it brought elation and joy, a sense of being whole again, even if it wasn't going to lead anywhere this time. It gave her hope for the future.

Tired of posing, Kade returned to her side and gently took the camera from her hand. Their fingers met briefly, and their eyes locked as Chelsea felt that spark of electricity flow through her with the brief contact. He leaned in close to her ear, still having to shout to make himself heard.

"I heard a legend about this place. It was something along the lines of 'if you and your partner could run from one side of the falls to the other without getting wet, you would come out the other end automatically married.'"

His breath on her neck made her tremble, but she steadied herself and turned her head to reply. She had to place a hand on his shoulder to balance as she stretched to reach his ear to answer.

The innocent touch thrilled her, feeling far more intimate than it should. She inhaled his scent as he tilted his head down to her mouth to assist her. Despite the headiness of the moment, she kept her words down to earth.

"We both know that's hogwash, it's a temple wedding or nothing!"

Kade straightened and laughed at her words, and Chelsea removed her hand from his shoulder, feeling the loss of the firm warmth beneath her palm immediately. He leaned back down toward her.

"Since its hogwash, why don't we give it a try? Fun challenge."

He stepped back to look at her, waiting for an answer. She thought it over, not mentioning the version of the myth that she had heard. True or not, it might be fun to try; the worst that could happen was that they would get wet.

She grinned and nodded at him and he packed his camera back into its waterproof case and tucked it into his pack. He held out a hand to her and she took it willingly, the gesture meaning much more to her than it did to him. They made their way to the bottom of the falls, where they both laughed as they looked at the water.

The rock behind was sheer cliff face with no crevices or caves to duck into and avoid the relentless, crashing flow. There wasn't even really a gap between the water and the jutting rocks. They would have to just run directly through the rushing fall or inch their way along the rock face—either way, they were getting soaked!

"Impossible," Chelsea yelled, exaggerating the word so he could lip-read it.

He nodded and shrugged, then gave her a wicked grin, his eyes sparkling with excitement. He grabbed her hand and raised his eyebrow. She laughingly nodded and he squeezed, the gesture constricting her heart as much as her fingers. He took a sprinter's stance and she knew they were going for the run. She had to admit it was crazy, but it was a fun, carefree crazy, and it felt great.

They took off, Kade taking the lead but keeping a firm grip on her hand as they entered the flow. The water instantly soaked them and pummeled down on them like the world's greatest power shower. Bent almost double under the force, they were gasping for breath through their hysterical laughter as they scrambled for the other side.

Almost clear of the falls, disaster struck. Chelsea slipped and fell, landing badly with her right foot twisted beneath her. Kade ground to a halt as he felt the tension on his arm, her fall almost jerking him backward. He turned and looked at her, shocked and afraid as she tried to get to her feet, but the shooting pain through her ankle caused her to collapse back onto the ground.

Kade bent over and scooped her up into his arms with ease, carrying her from under the torrent. With her cradled gently in his arms, he made his way to the pool of water that gathered at the base of the falls, placing her gently on the edge. He was constantly muttering, but she couldn't make out the words.

She instinctively reached to undo her hiking boot in order to relieve some of the pain, but Kade placed a hand over hers, shaking his head. Instead, he took her booted foot and plunged it into the water, ensuring it was submerged up to her calf, covering her ankle.

"Can't take the boot off," he yelled. "If it swells too much, we won't get the boot back on. The water isn't that cold, but hopefully it's cold enough to maybe stop or slow down the swelling and the bruising."

Chelsea nodded. He was right, of course; she didn't know what she was thinking, about to remove her boot like that. She sat with her foot in the water, feeling like an idiot. She could feel some of the pain lessening, wishing the water were icy enough to numb her ankle completely.

Kade looked utterly miserable, and she felt dreadful that she had ruined his day. She felt even worse when he left her there, going off to look around in various directions. Upon returning, he sat down heavily beside her, a look of defeat on his face.

"I can't find a route where I'd be able to carry you safely all the way down," he shouted. Chelsea shook her head, the volume of the falls too loud to explain what she wanted to say.

She put her hands over her ears indicating she couldn't hear him, and then she struggled to get up. Catching her meaning, he lifted her into his arms again and walked with her far enough from the falls so they could hear each other talk.

"I don't need you to carry me, I can walk."

"You can't."

"Well, maybe not, but I can hobble," she grinned, trying to cheer him up. Her attempts failed.

"Maybe I can call someone to come and get you down; we need to get you to the emergency room."

"Don't be silly, I don't need to go to the hospital. It's just a bad sprain at worst, maybe not even that. All it needs is an ice pack and elevation and it'll be fine by morning."

"I'd be happier if we got it checked out. What if it's broken?"

"Believe me, I know a broken bone when I feel it. Honestly, it's not that serious."

"I'm so sorry, Chelsea, I was a complete idiot."

"We were both complete idiots, and it was fun. This is just a minor inconvenience. I'm sorry I ruined your day."

He looked at her incredulously. "You have *not* ruined my day. It's me that has ruined yours with my reckless and harebrained ideas."

"Okay, let's just agree that we are a couple of fools and apportion blame equally."

"Fine, for now. We'd better address the immediate issue of getting you off this mountain. Can you walk at all?"

"I don't know."

Chelsea tried to take a step but her ankle gave way instantly. Kade quickly caught her, putting an arm around her waist and supporting her.

His toned body felt really good pressed against hers, and she wrapped an arm around him, allowing him to take some of her weight as she limped and hopped along. His proximity was worth the pain, and she found herself almost glad of the injury as an excuse to have him hold her this way.

"I don't think you'll make it all the way like this. Maybe I could carry you across some parts."

"We don't actually need to go down the mountain," she admitted. "If you look over to your left, do you see that building tucked into the hillside?"

Kade peered in the direction she indicated. "Yes, I do. A building means a road, right? We can work our way over, then flag down help."

"We won't need to, I live there."

"You live…wait a minute. You live on a mountain. This mountain?"

"Sure do."

"Why didn't you say so before? Let's get you home and get that ankle packed in ice."

Kade swung her into his arms again and began walking, keeping his concentration on the ground underfoot as he navigated his way in the direction of the block of condos. Despite the jostling, Chelsea found it a very enjoyable ride.

She snuggled against his chest, feeling as if she belonged there, as if she had always been there. On a few occasions, he needed to put her down so they could navigate a trickier part together, but as soon as they were clear, she was back in his arms.

All too soon (as far as Chelsea was concerned), she was digging in her pocket for her apartment keys. Unlocking her door and swinging it open, Kade carried her indoors. She directed him to the kitchen where he placed her gently onto one of her chairs.

She caught his frown as he spotted the fleece jacket, hung over the back of another chair at her dining set. She blushed, knowing how untidy it looked. She had left it there deliberately, serving as a reminder of the moment she had realized she was moving on, almost like a visual affirmation to herself to keep things that way, looking forward and not back.

"Do you have a medical ice pack?" Kade was asking her as he rummaged in her freezer.

"Um, no, I don't think so."

"Bag of frozen peas?"

She laughed. "No."

He turned around to face her. "Dish towel?"

"Second drawer."

"Glass?"

"Shelf on the top right."

He busied himself filling a glass with ice from the icemaker in the refrigerator door, then dumping it into the towel he had found and laid out, folding it up so the ice wouldn't burn her skin. "Let's get that boot off while we still can."

She watched as he knelt in front of her, unlacing her hiking boot, easing it off. He was coming across as efficient, perhaps even gruff, but the tenderness in his action as he gently eased the boot and her thick sock free and examined her ankle belied his bedside manner.

Ugly purplish and black bruises had already begun to form on the surface of skin over the ankle bone, and she heard him gasp as he looked at it. She winced but didn't complain as he prodded it carefully, trying to assess the damage.

"I think you're right, I don't think it's broken, but we'd know for sure with an x-ray. Won't you change your mind?"

"No, honestly, it's not necessary."

"Okay, if you insist," he muttered, obviously frustrated by her stubbornness.

He went through to the sitting room, returning with a cushion from her sofa. Arranging another one of the kitchen chairs in front of her, he placed the cushion on it and then slowly lifted her leg so the heel of her foot rested comfortably on the pillow.

Next, he rolled her trousers up as far as her calf, and Chelsea mentally high-fived herself for having shaved her legs that morning. She couldn't imagine the embarrassment she would feel right now if she hadn't. She giggled at the mental image and Kade frowned at her.

"Are you all right? You're not going into shock or anything?"

Chelsea shook her head and grinned sheepishly at him. "No, just a thought I had."

"Care to share?" he asked as he retrieved the ice pack and pulled up another chair beside her foot. He sat down and applied the ice to her bruised and swollen ankle.

"No, not really," she replied, letting out a sharp hiss as the cold hit the hot, throbbing injury.

"Sorry," he grimaced, realizing it was uncomfortable for her. "But it's the best thing to do, and I have to hold it here for quite some time, so you may as well entertain me with those thoughts."

"You don't have to stay; you've done more than enough."

"You're not getting off that easily, so don't argue. I'm staying until I see some of this swelling go down and you being able to move around on your own."

His tone let Chelsea know he wasn't going to stand for any arguments, so she decided to sit back and enjoy his company and the glorious view while she could.

"Oh, did you ever get around to reading that manuscript we talked about?" she suddenly thought to ask, glad to turn the conversation to something work-related to distract from how wonderful it was to be spending a Saturday with him and to have him here in her home.

The thought surprised her. Considering this had been her sanctuary guarding her from the pain of the outside world for so long, and how she had hesitated to accept even Carter into the fortress, she hadn't given a single thought to allowing Kade to enter.

Bearing in mind he was the very one she had subconsciously feared the most, it was quite a revelation.

"I did, and I loved it, but you're right, a marketing nightmare!"

They laughed together. "Have you managed to come up with anything?"

"Well, look, I don't really talk about things this early on. I often get ridiculous ideas into my head to begin with and play around with them. They are often discarded, but they can lead to something great. Do you know what I mean?"

"Of course, you're brainstorming, throwing every idea out there, but doing it alone."

"Yeah, so that's where I am."

"Tell me," she urged gently.

"Promise you won't laugh?"

"Only if you're laughing with me," she grinned at him.

"Fair enough, I guess. The first thing I did was to contact the other departments and ask if they had anything similar, something they thought the company should really handle but were unsure of where to place it.

"It turned out there were quite a few, and several great ones. I thought about doing a single campaign to cover them all, hoping that maybe everyone could pull them together in time for a Christmas push."

"That sounds like a good idea so far—one advertising campaign to promote several books across a variety of genres is perfect for the holiday market."

"I thought so too. As I was thinking it over, sci-fi with a topping of romance and a side of religion, historical with a portion of fantasy, children's with sexual morals…hey, don't look at me like that. It's good, really good. It's all done with gently-disguised euphemisms and subtle connotations, totally suitable for a kid's first novel, but reading it as an adult, you can see the deeper underlying theme, and it really does plant the seeds for living a faithful, monogamous lifestyle.

"You should give that one a read sometime. Anyway, it all sounded like a weird menu, like foods that shouldn't go together but do. Peanut butter and jelly, French fries and ice cream, fish fingers and custard."

Chelsea laughed, her knowledge of sci-fi easily allowing her to pick up the reference of his last example. "You like sci-fi?"

He nodded. "I sure do. So what I came up with first was the mishmash of things in Christmas stockings or under the tree, hence why I thought of a Christmas campaign, like giving two presents in one with these books. Then considering the menu theme, I thought about maybe using a play on a very famous slogan, one that sells food from an establishment that allows you to mix and match a huge menu."

"Okay," Chelsea grinned. "I see where you're going with this. Any slogans yet?"

Kade blushed, muttering about it being very rough and not that good yet before taking a deep breath. "Do you want surprise with that?"

Chelsea's laughter peeled throughout around the cozy kitchen.

"Hey! You promised not to laugh!" Kade mock protested, not being able to help but join in with her.

"I'm sorry," she gasped. "I'm laughing in a good way, honest! It's a million miles away from anything we have ever done before, but I actually love it. I can see the billboards already, the slogan with the books poking out of the top of a similar box, packed like fries. I think Mom might go bananas though."

"You don't think Grace will go for it? I already said it was just my initial idea, I—"

"Don't be too quick to discard it. I think it's exactly what we need to hit with a punch and raise the company profile. Everyone will be talking about it, and that's always a good thing.

"If Courtney likes it, then the two of us could certainly persuade Mom. She's got a soft spot for Courtney and gives in to her a lot." Chelsea winked conspiratorially at Kade, and he smiled back at her."

"I don't want to bulldoze my new employer into something she doesn't like, but if you like it, then I'll certainly do some mock-ups and present it to her."

They talked over the marketing concept for another hour, and eventually Kade inspected her ankle once again. "Looks like the swelling has gone down some, but you need to keep it raised and iced right up until the last minute. Do you have anything in the house that might help you move around when absolutely necessary?"

Chelsea thought hard, eventually coming up with an idea. "I've got ski poles; not ideal, but probably the best I can do."

Kade nodded. "Not bad, they'll do in a pinch. Where are they?"

"In the back bedroom closet."

Kade disappeared and Chelsea sat back, contented. Being incapacitated was a small price to pay for such an amazing day and the pleasure of being with Kade for this length of time.

Despite the excitement she felt in his presence, they shared a deep sense of companionship that was usually only achieved after knowing someone for a long time. Whatever had been up with him this morning, he was back to his normal, cheerful, easygoing self now.

She had to eat her thoughts when he returned carrying the ski poles. He laid them down then silently removed the ice pack, carrying it through to the sitting room.

He motioned for her to get up and come through. She struggled to get to her feet, awkwardly trying to let the bendy poles take a little of her weight and help her balance.

What happened to change things?

She made it to her couch, sitting down heavily. Once there, Kade pulled the coffee table over to her and placed her foot there, on top of the cushion he had rescued from the kitchen. He placed the pack around her ankle and stood up straight.

"Well, I've hung around longer than I should, so I guess I'll be going. Thanks for the vote of confidence on my idea, and I hope your ankle gets better soon. If you're not able to go to work on Monday, you can explain to Grace it was my fault. I could arrange for my assistant to drop by with anything you need if you want."

Chelsea felt very small and very crushed. Kade was suddenly back to being professional and distant, polite and helpful but detached.

"It's all good." She tried not to let her disappointment show. "I can organize that by myself if necessary. I'm sure I'll be fine by then. Thanks for rescuing me from the mountainside and bringing me back home."

"You're welcome," he said, turning to leave without another word.

As she heard the door click shut behind him, Chelsea reached for her cordless phone from the side table. Pressing the button to dial the pre-stored number, she couldn't wait for Grace to answer.

"Hey, Mom, it's Chelsea. How are you?"

Chelsea went on to tell her Mom all about the team-building day, explaining how great Stephen had turned out despite the dubious start.

They discussed the exercises and what she felt she had learned in detail. Eventually, Chelsea got down to the point of the call, explaining her injured ankle and how she was worried she wouldn't make it to church the next day.

"I'm sure everyone would understand, but if you really insist on being there, I have a plan. Remember when Carter broke his leg when he was twelve trying to jump Sunset around our course?"

"I certainly do," Chelsea grinned, cheered up and comforted as always by a conversation with her mom. "He was one feisty Arabian; no way was he jumping anything he didn't want to jump."

"Exactly, but Carter being Carter wouldn't listen, had to find out the hard way. Anyway, I still have his crutches here somewhere, and I'm sure they were adjustable. I'll pick you up in the morning and bring them with me. You could freeze a bandage and wear it for going out, since you'll have to take the ice pack off. Maybe you should stay with me until you're back on your feet so I can help you out."

"I'll gladly accept the ride and the crutches. I'm not sure if it will be necessary to stay; I'm sure I'll be fine soon."

"We'll play it by ear on that one then, but you're always welcome here. So how did this injury come about? You were always so sure-footed when climbing."

"I wasn't exactly climbing at the time."

Chelsea went on to explain what she and Kade were doing when she fell, quick to add how apologetic he had been and how gallantly he had carried her almost all the way home and stayed with her, taking care of her.

"I suppose we were all young and reckless at one point," Grace sighed. "How are things between you two now?"

"Well, at first he seemed kind of distant, almost as if he was avoiding me. As the day went on, things got much easier and he was back to his normal self, but then just before he left, he pulled away from me again, withdrawing completely.

"I don't understand it, Mom. I actually thought he might like me, but since I've admitted to myself that I like him, he's backed off. Maybe I'm giving off the wrong vibe, coming across too forward."

"He does like you, Chelsea. It's been quite obvious to pretty much everyone in the firm. I can't explain his recent actions either. I really can't see it being you; you aren't exactly the type to throw yourself at someone."

"No, I guess not." Chelsea sighed. "I really like him though, Mom. Not only is he gorgeous and very 'eligible,' as you put it, but we get on so well—it's as if we've known each other for years. We can talk for ages; even silence is comfortable with him.

"The only thing that's awkward between us is how I feel about him. I know I could fall in love with him so easily; in fact, I might already be half-way there after today."

"Maybe he just needs some time to adjust. After all, you are probably treating him differently than you did when you met."

"I wish that was all it was. No, he came right out and said that he had hopes of us dating, but now he knew it wasn't going to happen."

"Oh, Chelsea, I'm sorry."

"Don't worry, Mom, I'm fine with it. As much as I want it to be him, want *him* in fact, this whole experience has opened me up to love again. It's shown me I still have the capacity for it, and stopped me from being frightened of getting hurt.

"Even if I never fall in love with anyone else, it's been a lesson I needed to learn and I'm thankful for it. I know my prayers tonight will include my thanks for putting Kade in my path, in whatever capacity."

"I'm so glad you can see things that way, and so glad to have you back in one piece. You know what we always say—whatever is meant to be will be. Everything works out the way it's meant to."

"Thanks, Mom. I'll see you tomorrow."

"Take care, darling. Keep that ankle rested and I'll see you in the morning."

Hanging up the phone, Chelsea settled back. Stuck as she was, she might as well do some reading. Thank heavens there was always a pile of manuscripts on every table in every room.

CHAPTER ELEVEN

As spring turned to summer and summer to fall, the company was in high gear trying to ensure that everything was in place for Christmas.

Courtney was fully on board with the "menu campaign," as it had been nicknamed, and the three of them had sold the idea to Grace. She was a little concerned it was too down-market to begin with, but she had eventually agreed that something frivolous and fun might be good for the company to try, especially for the holidays.

Chelsea had spent a lot of time in Kade and Courtney's company as they worked together on how best to present the concept, and with each moment she spent with him, she had to admit she was falling a little deeper down the rabbit hole of emotions.

They now considered each other good friends, and Kade would often call on her to accompany him for lunch or talk over ideas, but he had never mentioned dating again or given any indication that he would like to.

Chelsea learned to live with the limitations of their relationship, although she secretly longed for so much more. She still couldn't control the excitement she felt whenever she saw him, the uncontrollable grin that broke out whenever she thought of him or spoke of him. He still caused her chest to constrict and butterflies to dance in her tummy every single time he walked into a room, but she accepted it would get her nowhere.

She couldn't hide the electricity that sparked when they touched, though, and often wondered if he felt it too. If he did, he was doing a better job of concealing his reaction than she was.

Thinking about Kade and fantasizing about a future together had become a favorite pastime of Chelsea's, and it was the one she was engaged in when the familiar tap on her office door broke her reverie.

"Come in," she called, the smile already spreading across her face.

Kade's sculpted and masculine face popped around her door. "It's Friday, almost the weekend, you up for lunch with a lonely ad man today?"

"Sure," Chelsea laughed, marking her place in the manuscript she was working on and rising from her desk.

His reference to being lonely made her wonder about his love life. He was probably one of the most gorgeous men to walk this planet, and several of the single girls in the firm would have fallen over themselves to queue up for the chance of a date, but he hadn't shown interest in any of them.

She had to admit that she was glad about that; it would have been hard for her to learn that he was seeing one of her colleagues, but she was also curious as to why he would remain isolated when so many opportunities were open to him. Halfway through the meal, she decided to raise the issue.

"So tell me, why are you still a lonely ad man?"

Kade paused with a forkful of food almost to his mouth. "Been too busy to make friends," he shrugged, taking the bite of food.

"That's not what I meant. I just wondered why you haven't been on any dates. I know you spend all weekend working."

"Says the girl that carries armfuls of files out to her car every night," he snorted, giving her a playful finger wag.

"Touché, but we're not talking about me. What I mean is how come you haven't dated anyone since you arrived?"

She was amazed at both her boldness, and her willingness to set herself up for pain if she found out that he had been dating all along, but she had to satisfy her curiosity on the matter. Kade looked slightly uncomfortable at the turn the conversation had taken, and he hesitated before answering.

"I really haven't been anywhere except work, church and home. There hasn't been any opportunity to meet anyone," he mumbled, keeping his eyes on his plate.

"So you wouldn't date anyone from work? Is that a self-imposed rule you have set for yourself, no mixing business with pleasure?" Chelsea picked at her food, moving it around the plate as she asked, nervously waiting for him to answer.

"No, I have no problem with that at all. I guess none of them have caught my eye."

"You're kidding! There are lots of pretty girls that work in the firm, and a large percentage of them belong to our church. I can name at least twenty who would love to go on a date with you," she chuckled, knowing full well she would secretly include herself in that list.

Kade deliberately placed his fork on the side of his plate and leaned back in his chair. He caught her eye and held her gaze, a serious expression on his face. "I agree there are many pretty women there, and several are really nice, but that's not enough for me to ask them on a date.

"You may think I'm a hopeless, pathetic romantic seeking something that only exists in books and movies, but I'm not the kind of guy who is looking for a few enjoyable nights out, or hopes that something will be a slow burn. I absolutely believe that when I find the girl for me, there will be an immediate connection, an instant spark, and I'll know for sure she is the woman I want to spend the rest of my life with.

"Until then, I don't see the point of dating for the sake of dating. Does that sound crazy?"

"Absolutely not, I totally agree!" Chelsea replied enthusiastically.

"Was that how it was with your boyfriend?"

"Yes, mostly," she replied carefully. "As a member of the church I'd known him since I was young. I used to say that I was going to marry him, in a childlike way. Then one day, when we were a little older, we looked at each other and just knew that it had been true all along."

"So you were childhood sweethearts. That must have been nice."

Chelsea thought she could detect a slight edge to his voice, but it was so heavily concealed with sadness that she couldn't discern its meaning.

"It was," she said softly. "I'm sure you'll find it too one day."

He smiled ruefully at her. "So is he coming into town this weekend?"

"Who?" Chelsea asked, confused at the sudden change of subject.

"Your boyfriend."

"Oh, I see. No, I'm afraid he won't be coming to town ever again. Clark died."

"What? Oh heavens, I'm so sorry, I hadn't heard. But you haven't been off work or…."

"It's okay Kade, it was over two years ago," she interrupted, trying to relieve him of the obvious distress he felt.

"But I saw him just the week before the team-building course."

The confusion was plastered all over his face and mirrored on Chelsea's, who was trying to figure out how Kade could have possibly seen Clark or even know who he was.

"Wait, back up a minute, I think we're confusing each other here. I'm talking about my fiancé, Clark, who was a soldier and was killed in Afghanistan over two years ago now. Who exactly are you talking about?"

"Umm, the guy you were so happy to see in your office, the one who literally swept you off your feet in my presence, of course."

Chelsea racked her brain, hoping to clear the muddle the conversation had caused in there, desperately trying to recall the moment to which he was referring. Realization dawned on her and her face went white with shock.

"You mean the day Carter turned up out of the blue?"

"I don't know what his name is, but you seemed pretty close."

"Oh, Carter and I are very, very close," she replied, her eyes twinkling. Things were starting to make a lot more sense to her now. "I love my brother, my *twin* brother, very much."

Chelsea couldn't help but burst out laughing at the emotions that crossed Kade's face, everything from shock, relief, and embarrassment flitting across his handsome features as he took in her words.

"You honestly didn't notice the resemblance?" she chortled, delighted at having him back on his heels as he had done to her so many times, without even realizing it. It was exciting to have the chance to tease him. *Paybacks are so much fun!*

"No, all I saw was the woman I might have a chance of falling in love with in the arms of another man."

Chelsea's laughter died in her throat, her pulse racing and her heart pounding in her chest as if it were trying to break free from her rib cage and soar to the ceiling. "What did you just say?"

Kade reached over and placed one of his large, strong hands over hers. "I'm sorry; I shouldn't have blurted that out. Chelsea, I have been such an idiot. When I first walked into that interview room and saw you, I felt the very thing I have waited to feel all my life. I instantly felt drawn to you, was desperate to get to know you.

"Sparks flew every time I was near you; and when we touched, I felt like my heart had stopped and someone was shocking me to get it beating again.

"I tried so hard to get to the stage where I could ask you out, but you kept me firmly at arm's length, despite my best efforts."

"I'm sorry about that, I can explain—"

"You don't have to explain, and I want to say this before I lose the courage. Everyone I asked said you were single, but then I saw you with...well, your brother actually. I thought he had to be a boyfriend, and all my dreams were shattered in that moment.

"Then you said you'd had an overnight guest and I put two and two together and came up with a hundred and five. I found it so hard to believe that you would allow that—I mean you're a Carpenter, and you're all held in such high regard at church and in the community. Everything was screaming that I was wrong.

"In my heart, I knew you weren't that kind of girl, but the facts in front of me were telling me otherwise. Then when I saw the jacket at your apartment, then the pieces of men's clothing and the photograph of you with a completely different guy, well, I was heartbroken.

"I had to admit to myself that not only were you unavailable to me because you were with someone else, but there wasn't even hope left because I thought you weren't worthy to be married in the temple."

Chelsea couldn't help but giggle. She had never heard anyone sound so remorseful and, well, almost pitiful in his desire to be forgiven.

He had hung his head, unable to look her in the eye as he explained how he had come to misjudge her so badly, but now he looked up at her again, hope beginning to shine. "You're not mad at me?"

"No, I don't think so. I'm a little shocked to be considered a scarlet woman; I have to say that's a first! I do understand how those things might have looked and how you came to the conclusions you did, though.

So was that why you were so distant with me on the morning we went hiking, because you thought I was involved?"

"Yes, I already had feelings for you, so pulling away and keeping you distant was only my way of trying to protect my heart, to stop myself from getting in any deeper. It didn't work, as you can probably tell."

"At least now I know why you said you couldn't ask me out, and why you left so abruptly after bringing me the ski poles. It's all making sense now."

"I can't apologize enough; I acted like a complete idiot. I let my head rule over my heart and ignored what I knew to be the truth."

"So if you thought I was so...immoral, how come you wanted to still be friends?"

The question was more of a test than a desire for answers. Chelsea wanted to be with someone who shared her values and was willing to talk openly about them to those that wanted to learn, but she didn't want to be with someone who was judgmental, or looked down on others for not sharing their values.

She had met plenty of those in her life, from all different religions, and she didn't feel it was a Christian way to live.

Now that she had broken down her inner barriers, she wanted to experience life again, integrating and mingling with all sorts of people in a range of situations and activities. Just because there were things she didn't do, didn't mean she had to shun others who did.

"You know it's not for us to judge, Chelsea. There was no way I was cutting someone out of my life just because they indulge in activities that I don't feel are right for me.

"Each of us must listen to what we think God is telling us, and whether we choose to comply is an individual choice made of our own free will.

"Although a relationship and a future with you would have been impossible, it didn't change who you were—a beautiful, funny, smart, creative woman whose company I enjoyed. As much as I told myself I should stay away, I just couldn't. If friendship was all I could have, I wanted every ounce of it."

Chelsea nodded, the answer being the one she had hoped he would give.

"Now it's my turn to explain a few things. After Clark was killed, I shut down completely. I cut myself off from everybody and took refuge up on the mountain. I barricaded my heart against love because I couldn't stand the pain it brought.

"When I saw you at your interview, it was the first time I was attracted to a man since Clark—the only other man apart from Clark, in fact. That scared the living daylights out of me!

"I knew I had to strengthen my shields and keep my distance. The more I got to know you and know about you, the harder that became and the more scared I was, not to mention the more guilty I felt for dishonoring Clark. That's why I was so mean to you."

"Why did you stop being mean to me?" Kade smiled and squeezed the hand he still held, taking the edge off the words, letting her know that he didn't think that way but was only using her expression.

"With the help of Carter, my Mom, and more importantly, God, I realized that by cutting love from my life and running from even the mere possibility, I was only half alive, not to mention straying from a path I was perhaps meant to walk.

"I decided I had to embrace my feelings and learn the lessons, no matter where they led or if it caused me more heartache. That's when I let my barriers down and got to know you."

"Chelsea Carpenter, did I just hear you say that you might have feelings for me?"

"Kade Richardson, I do believe you did."

They both grinned, their smiles softening and their eyes filling with warmth and emotion as they gazed at each other, Kade still clutching Chelsea's hand across the table.

"I think we have both learned some very valuable lessons here, ones that we really needed to learn."

"I couldn't agree more; it seems we have more in common than we thought," Chelsea agreed.

"In that case, would you do me the honor of coming out on a date with me?"

"I'd be delighted to."

Chelsea's words were restrained, belying the feelings inside her. Her tummy fizzled with anticipation and delight, her heart felt like it was Zumba dancing in her chest.

She wanted to jump up and down and scream with delight through the restaurant. She wanted to grab random people in the room and waltz around with them, yelling, "He asked me out!" at the top of her lungs, sharing her joy with everyone within her range.

She had longed for this moment, and now it was actually here. She brought herself back down to earth, promising herself she would let her exuberance loose once she was in the privacy of her condo.

"Since we've both been idiots and wasted so much time, how does tomorrow sound? Is that too short notice?"

"On the contrary, it sounds too long to wait. How about tonight?"

Kade threw his head back and laughed. Neither he nor Chelsea noticed the other diners smiling at the young couple who were having such a good time. They were too wrapped up in each other to notice the stares.

"Your wish is my command, m'lady," Kade said with mock gallantry. "Tonight it is. What shall it be— into the city for a trip to the theatre, a late dinner at Aria Trattoria?"

Chelsea grimaced, not fancying the stuffy setting and expensive restaurant he had named. She enjoyed those things occasionally, but she wanted tonight to be about getting to know Kade, being relaxed and comfortable with him in a setting where she felt at home.

"How about we go for a movie and dinner afterward at Sundance?"

Kade was visibly relieved at her suggestion. "A girl after my own heart! I really wanted to suggest that but I thought it sounded too casual for a first date."

Chelsea shook her head. "No, for us, it's perfect."

"Great! I'll pick you up at 7:00 if that's okay?"

"Perfect, but make it at the homestead and not my apartment."

"Sure. Oh my goodness, look at the time! If we don't get back to work, we're both going to be fired!" he exclaimed as he withdrew his hand and rose to leave, rushing round the table to pull Chelsea's chair out for her.

"Don't worry," she winked at him. "I'm sure the boss will show some leniency just this once, given the circumstances."

"I sure hope so," he laughed, taking her hand as they walked out of the restaurant together.

CHAPTER TWELVE

"What do you think?"

Chelsea stood awkwardly in front of the female members of her family, unsure of the outfit she had chosen from the array that her sisters had helped her pull from the closet, offering them up as possibilities and vocally expressing their varied opinions.

"I think it's perfect," Courtney declared. "Not too stuffy and rigid, and cashmere is perfect for a casual first date. It says class and effort, but not effort to the point of desperation, like you've tried but not tried too hard."

"The green of the sweater really brings out the green flecks in your eyes, Honey. You look great." Her mother smiled at her.

"Thanks everyone, thanks for helping out. I'm so nervous!"

"What's the big deal? It's only a date!"

As always, Courtney couldn't see what the fuss was about, having a unique way of taking life in her stride with ease. As far as Courtney was concerned, nothing was ever a big deal.

Chelsea sighed, wondering how she could explain it. "It's my first date in a long, long time. Once you're in a relationship with someone that you know is the one, and you think it's going to be for the rest of your life and eternity beyond, spending time with them is just that—it doesn't feel like going on dates anymore. I went from knowing Clark to going out with Clark.

"This is my first date with anyone else but him. I feel like a high school kid again, the shy girl snagging a date with the jock and not being able to believe it."

"It'll be absolutely fine; you'll have a great time. You're already friends with Kade the way you were with Clark," Cassie soothed.

Chelsea had headed straight back to her family home after work, way too excited to be alone and desperate to share her news. They had flocked around her, knowing something was up by her unexpected and unannounced appearance.

When Chelsea declared that she was going on a date with Kade that night, she had finally been able to release some of her overzealous excitement and exuberant joy as she danced around the family room with her sisters. They squealed like teenage cheerleaders as her mother and Maggie looked on, laughing at their antics.

Chelsea knew they were being childish and girly, that her feelings for Kade ran much deeper than her silly actions displayed.

Somehow, this was a culmination of everything she had lost—her love of romance, her childhood dreams, her ability to live life to the fullest, and her hope for the future. It had all been recaptured in this one moment of freedom with her sisters.

The high spirits continued as they had dragged her upstairs to help her figure out what to wear and talk dreamily about how handsome Kade was. Now with her outfit approved, there was nothing else to do but wait.

Clock watching was making her even more nervous and excited, so to pass the time, she explained the highlights of their lunch conversation.

Her delivery of the misunderstanding over Carter's identity caused them all much hilarity, and Chelsea knew that if Kade were to become a frequent visitor to the house, he would be teased about it forevermore.

She instantly pitied him, knowing how merciless her siblings could be when they had decent ammunition, and this most definitely fell within that particular category.

They all fell silent as they heard the approaching car. Glancing at the clock, Chelsea realized it was time. The hilarity fled and apprehension took over as she heard Nigel make his way to the door to answer the chimes.

Every nerve ending in her body tingled as she held her breath, waiting to see if it would be Kade that was announced as the caller.

As soon as he was led into the room, all her worries were gone, replaced by her sheer delight to see him. The expected butterflies arrived, as did the racing heart, but she was no longer concerned about those feelings, embracing them as the first twinges of love in a budding relationship. She stood to greet him and he presented her with a single red rose.

"You look beautiful, Chelsea," he almost whispered as he gazed at her, warmth and passion flaring in his ice blue stare.

She thanked him as she accepted the small gift, not noticing Maggie rushing out to fetch a vase for the flower. She did notice, though, the shared comedy moments between Courtney and Cassie as they pretended to swoon over Kade, but she only had eyes for him.

Grace cleared her throat gently and Chelsea was suddenly aware of the others in the room. "Please forgive me, where are my manners! Mom, you obviously already know, and this is my sister, Cassie, and you know Courtney. The man who let you in is Nigel, and this lovely lady with the vase is Maggie."

"It's a pleasure to meet you all. Good evening, Grace," Kade responded, having to tear his eyes away from Chelsea to acknowledge the others.

Chelsea reluctantly relinquished the rose to Maggie, who placed it in the water she had added to the vase and set it on the mantelpiece.

"Kade, we should get going; the movie starts at 7:30 and I'm a popcorn kinda girl."

"Oh, no! You mean you want me to stand in line at the concession stand for you? I think that might be too much to ask on a first date."

"No popcorn, no date," Chelsea said firmly, folding her arms and tapping her foot.

"Alright, I give in. I really want to see this movie," Kade joked as he held out an arm to escort Chelsea out to his car. "Have a good night everyone. It was great to meet you and I hope to see everyone again soon."

As they walked down the hall to the front door, Chelsea could still clearly hear her family.

"He's gorgeous," Cassie squealed. "I so have to use him in a book."

"It seems every man who enters this house will be in one book or another," Grace teased.

"He's not too bad at all. Seems like my sisters are all bagging themselves studs. Wonder when it will be my turn," Courtney added.

Even if she hadn't known the voice so well, Chelsea would have had no trouble identifying the member of the family who had made that little comment.

"Hmm, so I'm a stud am I?" Kade murmured so the others wouldn't hear, faking a lascivious look as he eyed Chelsea.

"Not a word I would use except when discussing the horses, but I wouldn't necessarily disagree with it."

They laughed together as they stepped out into the night. Chelsea didn't feel embarrassed by the moment at all. She felt so at ease with Kade, as if he had always been in her life, as if he was already part of her sometimes-loopy family—more correctly, her often-loopy family!

Besides, if he was going to be around as much as she wanted him to be, he had better get used to them fast.

"They're great," Kade said.

"I think so," she replied with a smile.

"But not as great as you," he added as he unlocked the car and opened the passenger door for her. He turned to her, taking both her hands in his, looking down at her, his face serious and gentle.

"Chelsea, you are the most beautiful, amazing woman I have ever known. I can't believe that I'm here with you now, about to spend the evening with you. It's a dream come true, one I've been waiting for all my life. I hope this night is the first of many."

"I hope so too, Kade," she replied, holding his gaze.

"I know I'm not supposed to do this until the end of the evening, but I've been longing to since the moment I first saw you, and I can't wait a minute longer."

Kade gathered her tenderly into his arms and bent his head to kiss her. All teasing and joking were forgotten as his lips met hers for the very first time. The kiss was tender and loving, Chelsea melting into his embrace as her knees went weak, and she felt dizzy in the headiness of the moment.

The intoxicating scents of the flower garden were carried to her on the warm, gentle breeze, the sounds of night creatures echoed in the stillness around them, and it was the most perfect kiss she could have ever imagined.

She expected fireworks to erupt behind them, birds to dance around them and an orchestra to begin to play. She wanted it to last forever, and she knew she was never going to let this man go.

As Kade softly broke the connection, he pulled her more tightly into his arms. She chuckled softly.

"What's funny?" he said lightly in her ear.

"I just had my Disney moment," she replied with a soft smile, tilting her head back to look into his face.

Kade pulled back to get a closer look into her eyes, mild curiosity on his face. "Is that a good thing?"

Chelsea laughed. "Only a man could ask such a question. Kade, it's the most amazing moment in the world, the one that every little girl dreams of having all her life."

"Good," he nodded, reassured. "Because I'm hoping that moments like those will be happening often, and for a very long time—hopefully for the rest of our lives and into eternity."

"Me too," she replied and he picked her up and swung her around in delight. This might be a first date, but they both knew it was so much more. He was laughing again as he set her back down beside the car.

"I'm glad we're on the same page there; I don't buy popcorn for just anyone, you know."

"I should think not, it's a very intimate gesture," she replied tartly as she slid into the passenger seat. "Get a move on! Hot, buttery deliciousness awaits."

"It would be ungentlemanly to keep a woman from her heart's desire," he commented as he slid into the seat beside her.

"Oh, I already have that. Now I want my popcorn."

They laughed together as they buckled up and headed for the movie, both overjoyed that this night was just the beginning of the rest of their lives together.

Now they both would find their sanctuary...in one another's arms.

Available Now – Book 3

Salvation, Courtney's Story

The Carpenter Chronicles, Book Three
Available now in paperback and ebook.

Excerpt from Book Three

She watched her sister swallow hard. "Okay, I wanted to ask you about tonight, you know, the *wedding* night."

Courtney frowned in annoyance as she suddenly realized what Chelsea was trying to ask. "You took Biology 101, too. You know where everything goes."

Chelsea sighed deeply. "I know the logistics of it, yes. I was hoping for a more personal take on it, things like how to be sexy, what to expect to feel, if it will hurt, that kind of thing."

Courtney's scowl deepened further and she was glad that Chelsea's eyes were covered. She absently retrieved an excess slice of cucumber and nibbled on it as she tried to contain her laughter.

"What makes you think I can tell you any of that?"

Chelsea's head whirled in Courtney's direction as the cucumber slices lifted as the eyebrows beneath shot upward. Chelsea sat up with a start, flinging the cucumbers slices to the floor.

"Oh, Courtney, I'm so sorry! I've misjudged this completely haven't I? It's just that you dated so much in high school and college, and you went out with Tom for such a long time, I just assumed …" her voice fell away, the despair at her incorrect assumptions apparent in the ending wail.

Courtney considered her words. *There's no denying I've dated a lot. I'd even concede that I began dating quite young, far younger than Grace had been happy about once she found out.*

Her early dates had an air of innocence about them, hands held under booths at the diner as they hung out there in groups, an arm around the shoulders in the movie theatre, maybe even a stolen chaste kiss before parting. Her later dates had been more adventurous, including beer downed at football games, and make-out sessions in cars parked at secluded viewpoints.

The thing was she never felt any of those sensual feelings when indulging in physical contact with her boyfriends, not even Tom. It wasn't that she considered her virginity anything special or something to be valued, she just hadn't ever felt turned on by them the way she thought she should be. So she'd felt there was no point in going any further with any of them.

The fact that other people made the same assumption about Courtney as her sister just did had saved Courtney from teasing, or even ridicule by her peers in high school and college.

* * *

Thinking it all over, she decided it was probably unfair of her to be angry with Chelsea for her assumption. In a much gentler tone, she attempted to put her at ease.

"I'm sorry, Chelsea, I've never gone all the way either, it's Mom you need to ask."

"Ewwww, no way!" Chelsea squealed, restoring the good humor of the room. "I guess we'll just have to fumble our way through, since it'll be the first time for both of us."

"I'm sure you'll both have a *lot* of fun finding out together," Courtney said suggestively, poking her sister and causing her to squeal and giggle again.

Just at that moment, Grace popped her head inside the door. "What's going on in here?" she asked as she stepped into the room.

"Nothing!" the girls replied in unison, then fell onto the bed in laughter.

Get SALVATION – Courtney's Story, A Christian Romance Here

Paperback and ebook: http://bit.ly/courtneybooks

Click here to be notified when other books become available.

IN CASE YOU MISSED BOOK ONE!

Sacrifice, Carrie's Story
The Carpenter Chronicles, Book One

Available now on Amazon.com and in bookstores.

Click here to order book one of the series.

If you've enjoyed reading this book, I really hope you'll leave some positive feedback on the Amazon sales page for it so other readers will know you liked it. It will really help get our Christian message out and I would so, so appreciate it. Just click here!

Janice

For updates on coming releases, sales and events for books by Janice Limb Myers, please sign up here:
http://JaniceLimbMyers.com

Support Christian Authors and Read Great Books: Christian Books in Multiple Genres, Join Christian Indie Author ~ Readers Group on Facebook for opportunities to learn about more great Christian authors.
https://www.facebook.com/groups/291215317668431/